ABOUT THIS BOOK

Every town has stories of its past, and Havenwood Falls is no different. And when the town's residents include a variety of supernatural creatures, those historical tales often become Legends. This is but one . . .

Ever since he was a young boy, Daniel McCabe and his family have been running to escape his father's past—a past scarred by the cruelty of humans against their kind. Indian reservations, the Japanese internment camps of World War II, and racial segregation only reinforce what he's been taught: humans mistreat those who are different. Fearing the same treatment if his shifter abilities are ever discovered, he keeps to himself and trusts very few. While the war may be over, the 1950s seem to be a time of conformity, and Daniel is anything but a conformist.

After Daniel moves his mom back to Colorado, the only place he has really considered home, a job opportunity brings him to a small town nestled in the Rocky Mountains. Havenwood Falls offers the promise of a new beginning—a chance to help the town grow and to establish a life for himself and for others like him. He even finds his mate.

Colleen Campbell is smart, funny, bold, and beautiful. And human.

Havenwood Falls has everything Daniel has dreamt about, offering a stable future with a woman he could love. But if he can't overcome everything he knows and believes, this fated beginning may already be at its end.

LEGENDS OF HAVENWOOD FALLS BOOKS

Lost in Time by Tish Thawer

Dawn of the Witch Hunters by Morgan Wylie

Redemption's End by Eric R. Asher

Trapped Within a Wish by Brynn Myers

Blood and Damnation by Belinda Boring

Fated Beginnings by E.J. Fechenda

Emeline by Katie M. John

Released From a Curse by Brynn Myers

A Pack of Lies by Kallie Ross

Kiss the Ashes by Desiree Lafawn

Hidden Truths by Colleen Nye

Wrath and Retribution by Belinda Boring

Changing Fate by Char Webster

Rise of the Witch Hunters by Morgan Wylie

The Drowning Bride by Seven Jane

Also try the main Havenwood Falls series; the YA line, Havenwood Falls High; the darker, sexier side of town, Havenwood Falls Sin & Silk; and the local supernatural college, Sun & Moon Academy.

Stay up to date at www.HavenwoodFalls.com

ALSO BY E.J. FECHENDA

THE NEW MAFIA TRILOGY

The Beautiful People

Clean Slate

Endings & Beginnings

Enforcer (a prequel novella)

THE GHOST STORIES TRILOGY

End of the Road

Havoc

The Triangle (Fall 2018)

HAVENWOOD FALLS

Fate, Love & Loyalty

HAVENWOOD FALLS HIGH

Fata Morgana

FATED BEGINNINGS

A LEGENDS OF HAVENWOOD FALLS NOVELLA

E.J. FECHENDA

Mom and Dad, thank you for everything. I love you.

CHAPTER 1

SUNSET CREEK, COLORADO AUGUST 1947

$\mathcal{D}$ust billowed out behind the truck, and the dirt road had grown increasingly bumpier and narrower the higher Daniel McCabe's dad drove up the mountain. The truck bounced over ruts and rocks, causing Daniel to bounce in his seat. The last sign of civilization he recalled seeing was a homestead with two sickly looking horses in the corral, emaciated to the point he could count the ribs. He had wanted to stop and give them his apple that was packed with his lunch, but his dad refused. He said there wasn't time to dillydally. He wanted to get to their destination before noon.

Judging by the sun high overhead, that time quickly approached. They passed a sign for Prospector Gulch, and Daniel noticed his dad's grip on the steering wheel tighten, as did the set of his jaw. Sheer determination pushed him forward on this task. When his dad asked him if he wanted to visit Sunset Creek, Daniel didn't hesitate to say yes. Sunset Creek had only been spoken about in whispers, accompanied by expressions of sadness. Daniel knew something bad had happened that had resulted in his grandfather dying, but he didn't know what. Now that they were approaching the old mining town, the place of his father's birth and his grandfather's death, hopefully he'd learn the whole story.

They rounded a bend in the road, and his dad slammed on the brakes, sliding to a stop on the dirt. An aspen tree lay on its side, blocking the way.

"Well," his dad said with a sigh, "looks like we're walking the rest of the way." He grabbed the satchel that contained their lunches and canteens of water before opening the door. Daniel scrambled out after him, eager to stretch his legs. They had been driving all morning. Sunset Creek was located in the mountains in Gunnison National Forest, about two hours west of where they lived in Colorado Springs. Daniel's dad was quiet as they marched along the narrow road so choked with overgrowth, it was hard to believe it was a road at all.

"Dad, how can anyone live out here?"

"Nobody does . . . anymore."

"Why?"

His dad paused and fished out a canteen from the bag. He screwed off the top, took a few deep gulps, and handed it over to Daniel. That's when he noticed his dad's hand was shaking. His dad didn't respond, just turned around and kept walking. Daniel easily kept up. Since he had turned fifteen three months ago, he had gone through a growth spurt. Now his long strides matched his dad's. The forest grew thicker around them, and it was so much quieter out here than in the city. Daniel itched to roam through the woods and smell everything. He was getting better at controlling his shift, and out here, where they hadn't seen any humans and he didn't detect any with his enhanced senses, the urge to be one with nature became increasingly difficult to contain.

As if sensing this, his dad grabbed his wrist. "Not yet," he said. "There will be time later."

Daniel let out a small growl, but nodded in understanding.

"I used to know these woods—they were like my second home once. Before . . ." His dad trailed off, staring off into the distance, but Daniel could tell he was lost in his thoughts. His forehead crinkled before he shook out of his trance and started moving again.

They walked side by side in silence until they reached an old wooden post. On the ground in front of it was a sign. The wood was half rotted, and the white paint faded to the point where some of the letters were gone, but he could still make out the words: Sunset Creek est. 1867. That was eighty years ago, he thought to himself as he took in what was left of the town laid out before him. There were structures left—a few homes and stores—but no sign of life. He could see where the mines had been carved out of the hillside above the town. Rusty machinery dotted the stripped earth. As they walked down the main street through the center of town, Daniel shivered as if ghosts followed them. Looking over at his dad, he could tell he was haunted by memories. Shells of buildings remained. Some of them were half burnt and leaning at a dangerous angle.

"Dad?" His voice shook with fear. "What happened here?"

"Humans. Humans happened." His dad's shoulders slumped as if exhausted, and he focused his blue eyes just past Daniel's shoulders. "Come, it's time you know. You're old enough."

He led them to the front steps of what was once the general store. The windows were busted out, glass littered the front porch, and the wooden door swung in the gentle breeze, rusty hinges letting out an occasional squeak. Once they were settled on the steps with sandwiches that his mom made in their hands, his dad started talking.

"Sunset Creek was a booming mining town in its heyday. The vein of gold they discovered made a lot of men rich. My father—your grandfather, Ian McCabe—arrived here from Ireland in 1875 with his oldest brother, Robert. Robert was seventeen at the time, and my father only thirteen. Even though it was a few years after the vein was first discovered, there was still plenty gold left for him to acquire some wealth.

"In 1878, Sunset Creek was still thriving. Even though the gold vein had been depleted, one of the largest silver veins had been discovered, attracting prospectors like bees to honey.

"As Sunset Creek grew, the boundaries encroached upon unclaimed land where wildlife was plentiful. Hunting and fishing provided a much-needed food source. According to what my father told me, in 1878, William Jenkins, a Sunset Creek resident, had gone out hunting with his twelve-year-old son, Johnny. He returned on the second day without any fresh kills. Instead, the bloody body he carried in his arms was his son. Johnny had been mauled by a mountain lion. William had shot the beast before it could snap his son's neck. A priest was brought in, and last rites were read at Johnny's bedside as he fought for his life. William and Judith Jenkins kept a vigil through the night. Fortunately, he survived, but there were more attacks by mountain lions. Your grandfather was one of the victims."

"What?"

"That's how he became a shifter. He was bitten. Imagine the shock and surprise when he first shifted."

"Holy Toledo!" Daniel sat back in awe. He'd always assumed his grandda was born a shifter like everyone else in his immediate family.

"The mountain lion attacks continued for several years, and multiple residents were bitten. Only after Johnny Jenkins shifted in public during an argument with his father, in front of the assayer's office, did your grandda figure out there were more mountain lion shifters like him. The reaction to Johnny's public change also made him realize he needed to be very careful about who knew his true nature."

"Why?" Daniel asked, leaning forward with his arms propped on top of his knees.

His dad sighed and ran a hand over his beard, which was a deep reddish brown that had only recently become threaded with some white hairs.

"Humans are easily afraid and easily suspicious of anyone they consider different. I mean, you've seen the reservations and the internment camps."

Daniel understood what he was saying. Even though the Second World War had ended two years earlier, pictures of Holocaust survivors that ran in newspapers were burned into his memory. Here in Colorado, the Japanese Internment camps, which the governor fought against, still existed. They were empty, the prisoners released to go back to their lives, but the structures remained as a reminder of how quickly people could turn against a whole group considered different or a threat.

"According to your grandda, it was late one night when a group of men who worked at the mines formed a mob. They had been drinking at the saloon and got riled up. Somebody mentioned Johnny Jenkins, and it escalated from there. They left the bar and marched down Main Street to the Jenkins house."

Daniel's dad paused and stared off across the street at the shell of what used to be the bar. A faded sign that read Silver Spur Saloon had come loose on one end and hung at an angle, partially blocking the doorless entrance. He swallowed once before continuing. "They burnt the fucking house down. Johnny and his family barely escaped."

Daniel's eyes widened, and his mouth hung open in shock, partly because of how horrible the story was, and also because his dad swore. He rarely said cuss words in front of him.

"Apparently, Johnny and his family left that night, and were never seen or heard from again, but things were different after that. Anyone who had been associated with them were cast under suspicion as well. My father kept hoping that things would settle down, but seeing a person transform into a wild animal is something people don't easily forget."

"But he stayed. I mean, you were born here. Why didn't he leave?"

He snorted, and his mouth twisted up in a smile. "Us McCabes are a stubborn lot," he said and winked at Daniel, who returned his grin. "He and his brother had settled in Sunset Creek and that's all they knew. They refused to leave. Also, I think love had something to do with it."

"Oh," Daniel responded with a knowing tone. "Gran."

"Yup. He met my mother, and she didn't have any desire to leave either."

Daniel scratched his head and swatted at a fly buzzing around his ear. The sun had shifted, and he was baking in its full afternoon heat. "Was Gran already a shifter when they met?"

"Yes. She had been bitten, too. As you are learning, we have enhanced senses, so it's easier to pick out nonhumans in a crowd. Soon the mountain lion shifters of Sunset Creek were holding their own gatherings in secret. These gatherings were the only way of exploring the animal side; they were a safe place."

Once again, his dad grew quiet and stared off into the distance. Daniel noticed his eyes shone with tears that never spilled. His dad cleared his throat and stood up. He paced in front of the steps where Daniel sat.

"When I was ten years old, I was with your grandda and gran and my sister at one of these gatherings. Now, mind you, the mines were almost depleted by this time and the population was growing smaller each month as people had to find work elsewhere. This also meant there were a lot of desperate people around. Desperate and angry people are like powder kegs waiting to go off. We thought our gatherings had gone unnoticed, but in a small town, it's hard to keep secrets. Unfortunately, someone noticed, and that was enough to light the fuse."

"What happened?" Daniel was leaning forward by now, completely engrossed in the story. He was finally going to learn what his dad and gran kept secret.

"They came for us. Tried to slaughter us all and came really close to succeeding." His dad's voice was rough with emotion, and he stopped pacing. With a sigh, he sunk down on the steps next to him. His shoulders were hunched over like he was physically burdened by the memory. "Homes were torched, friends were shot in the street . . . it was swift and brutal. I don't know how many survived. We scattered. My dad managed to get us to safety, urged us to head for the nearest town, and said that he'd catch up to us. He went back to fight, and we never saw him again."

Daniel shuddered as he absorbed the information. He had no idea his family history would be so dark. "Did you try to find him?" he asked.

"I wanted to go back and look for him, but your gran insisted we stay far away. She scoured newspapers for any coverage of the violence, but nothing was ever published. She thinks the government covered it up. It's possible. Just look at what's happening in New Mexico. That fellow found a spaceship on his farm, and now the news is saying it's a weather balloon. They probably are testing on aliens right now in some underground bunker. Hell, they probably captured a shifter or two and are testing them, too. All I know is Sunset Creek has been wiped from the map and was left to sink back into the earth. Humans can't be trusted, Daniel. Remember that. They can't handle anything out of the ordinary."

His dad's warnings were nothing new. Daniel had been hearing them his whole life, even more since his first shift, which took place three months ago, not too long after he turned fifteen. Now, knowing the history, he understood why.

He took his dad's warning to heart that day, adapting it as a rule that would follow him into adulthood: be careful who you trust, especially humans.

"I needed to tell you the history, Daniel. It's why we move so much. We can't afford to get too comfortable in one place. Your mother and I know it's been difficult, especially with you getting older."

The images Daniel's imagination conjured up flashed vividly through his mind, the carnage worse than any war movie playing at the local cinema. He pictured streets running red with blood and the empty street before him a scene of total chaos as shifters were slaughtered. His dad was right—he hated moving all the time. Just when he started to settle in and make friends, his family would pick up and move on. It had gotten to the point where he didn't bother making friends.

"Are we moving again?" Daniel asked, hoping to disguise the disappointment in his voice. His dad's expression said it all, in the tight set of his jaw and slight frown.

"I'm afraid so, son. This time we're heading east. West Virginia, to be exact."

Daniel's shoulders dropped, and he hunched over, curling inward and turning his head so his dad didn't see the tears welling in his eyes. It was worse than he could have imagined. Not only were they moving again, but they were leaving Colorado, the only constant—the only state he had always been able to call home.

Two weeks later, they left, Daniel crammed in the cab of the truck next to his mom, who sat in the middle. The truck's bed was piled high with their belongings, covered by a large black tarp to protect their things from rain.

The farther they drove, the more uneasy Daniel grew. He wanted to go back, felt it in his bones that they were heading in the wrong direction, but he was powerless to do anything, forced to follow his parents.

As they crossed the state line and entered Kansas, Daniel made a promise to himself: he would come back. As soon as he was able, he'd make his way back to Colorado.

CHAPTER 2

TEN YEARS LATER JUNE 1957

*D*aniel grabbed the paper sack of groceries, the bottles inside clinking with the movement. He thanked the cashier and started to leave the variety store that was on the corner of his street. He'd had a long day, and all he could think about was the cold six-pack of Coors he was carrying. His current foreman was a grade-A asshole who tested Daniel's temper. Fortunately, he had been training since he was a teenager to keep that temper in check. Sprouting claws or partially transforming into a mountain lion when he was surrounded by humans was a recipe for disaster.

He was about ready to leave the store when a flyer pinned to the community bulletin board caught his attention:

LOOKING FOR A CHANGE?
CONSTRUCTION FOREMAN NEEDED
MUST BE EXPERIENCED
MUST HAVE OWN TOOLS
Spend the summer in the mountains and be part of an exciting new opportunity.

Call 6-4511 for details and to apply.

Daniel unpinned the flyer and tucked it inside the bag. He *had* been looking for a change, and escaping the confines of the city appealed to him. With the prospect of something new ahead, his steps were lighter as he walked down the street to his apartment. Daniel and his mom lived on the bottom floor, while a young family lived upstairs in their two-story building. His mom, Margaret, was sitting out on the small porch, which was just large enough to accommodate the rocking chair she occupied. Late afternoon sun blanketed her in golden light, changing her hair from light brown to blond.

"Ah, there's my boy! Come sit, tell me about your day. Dinner will be ready in about ten minutes."

He complied and sat on the top stoop, stretching his long legs out in front of him. Dust covered his well-worn denim carpenter pants and his heavy boots. He paused for a moment with his eyes closed and his head tilted back as he scented the air and listened to the noises surrounding him. With his heightened senses, he could pick up so much more than a human. He could hear people talking two streets over, and he smelled someone grilling chicken, the sweet tang of barbecue sauce lacing the air. His stomach rumbled, and he opened his eyes. Reaching into the bag, he pulled out a beer. Holding the top against the railing, he smacked his hand hard on the cap, and it popped off, landing on the small patch of grass next to the walkway.

After a few long swallows, he sighed in contentment and grinned up at his mom. "What's for dinner?"

"Steak and potatoes. The potatoes are finishing up in the oven now. I made extra, in case you're hungry." She raised an eyebrow at him when his stomach rumbled.

"Thanks, Ma. I could eat a horse. It was a long day."

They chatted while he finished his beer, then went inside. As he pulled his beer out of the bag to put the rest of the bottles in the icebox, his finger brushed against the flyer, slicing his skin. He winced and examined the paper cut. It was small, only a tiny drop of blood bubbling to the surface. Shrugging, he stuck his finger in his mouth and sucked, shoving the flyer in his back pocket. For some reason, he didn't want to show his mom. Once he knew more and if he was offered the job, then he'd tell her. It would mean leaving her temporarily, but he knew she would be fine. She was strong, tough as nails, and had been through so much that he didn't want her to relocate with him. He'd send money back to take care of the bills that his dad's life insurance policy didn't cover.

"I'm going to go wash up before dinner," he told his mom, who was pulling potatoes out of the oven, and walked down the narrow hallway to his bedroom. Once inside, he stripped off his shirt, the fabric stiff with dried sweat, and tossed it in the hamper. The paper in his back pocket crinkled, reminding him of its presence. He pulled out and unfolded the flyer then immediately dropped it like it was on fire. The wording had changed.

COME BUILD YOUR FUTURE
AND HAVENWOOD FALLS' FUTURE
Call 6-4511 for details and to apply.

"Daniel, dinner's ready." His mom's voice drifted down the hallway. He lifted up the paper from the floor very carefully with two fingers and held it away from him like it was poisonous. He set it on top of his dresser and quickly left the room, needing time away to process what just happened. Maybe it was the beer on an empty stomach that was making him see things. That was the only logical explanation.

He was quiet during dinner, and his mom noticed.

"What's going on in that brain of yours?" she asked when she started to clear the table. "You hardly said a thing tonight."

"Mom, do you believe in magic?"

She paused and tilted her head to the side before answering. "Of course I do. Remember those witches who lived on our street in Pueblo? They cast some pretty incredible spells. Then there is us. I think a little magic was involved to create shifters. Why do you ask?"

Daniel chewed on his lower lip as he debated whether to tell her, but not one to keep secrets from his mom, he stood up.

"I'll be right back," he said and hurried to his bedroom. He grabbed the flyer, cautiously looking to see if the message had changed, but it was still the same. He strode into the kitchen and set it on the counter next to the stove with a dramatic flourish.

"What do you see?" he asked his mom.

She set the dish she was washing back in the sink and dried her hands on a towel before coming over to look. He watched her eyes dart as she read the brief summons.

"It's an advertisement for a construction job. Are you thinking about calling?"

"You don't see anything about building a future in Havenwood Falls?"

His mom frowned, deepening the lines around her mouth and the furrows in her forehead. She looked down at the sheet of paper again and slowly shook her head. She glanced up at him, her expression changing to one of concern. "Obviously you're seeing something different. Is that why you asked me about magic?"

Daniel let out an exasperated sigh and buried a hand in his thick, russet brown hair. He started pacing the length of the kitchen, a habit he learned from years of watching his dad do the same thing. "The original message was a generalized one for a construction foreman, like the one you are still seeing, but it's changed, for me. Holy cow, I sound crazy! Someone is going to lock me up in the booby hatch."

"Don't be ridiculous, Daniel. Come here and sit down."

His mom tucked her skirt behind her knees before she sat at the dinette table. The white top had already been scrubbed clean. The napkin holder and glass salt and pepper shakers stood in their usual place at the center. She lifted up the paper to the overhead light and examined it closely. Daniel sat down across from her and watched, his fingers tapping the table. She brought it close to her nose and inhaled deeply, her eyes briefly changing to their cat shape and flashing their bright amber color before turning back to human.

"There's something faint—an essence that's definitely magical in origin. I believe you, son. I think forces are at work here."

"Is it a trick, though? A trap by humans? Should I trust it?" He stood up and walked to the icebox, yanking on the chrome handle hard enough that the entire unit scraped forward on the floor. He slowed and took a deep breath. Even though he was home and away from humans, he couldn't get in the habit of displaying his strength. His father had taught him to always stay contained and control his emotions, which was easier said than done when he was a teenager. Now that he was twenty-five, it had become easier, but the rare display of his supernatural side, triggered by emotion, still happened.

He grabbed a beer and popped the cap off with his bare hands. Daniel didn't sit back down. His shifter side was itching to break free. It felt like the mountain lion was pacing just beneath his skin, its tail swishing from side to side with agitation.

"I think it would be highly unusual for humans to employ magic to lure you into a trap. Besides, we're fairly new to town, and we haven't given anyone any reason to suspect we're different. We've been so careful over the years."

What his mom said made sense. His dad had been so adamant that they move often enough to not raise suspicions. Daniel was raised to be as human as possible. When they did shift, to appease their other nature, his dad scouted out unpopulated and remote locations in advance. He and his mom continued all of these practices after his dad died. Did Daniel think his dad was a little paranoid at times? Yes, but he hadn't witnessed the horrors his dad had. They kept to themselves and interacted with humans only out of necessity. They didn't forge friendships with neighbors, because they were never in one place long enough. Daniel longed for a community, though, for relationships and for an existence that wasn't so . . . lonely.

"I'll admit I'm intrigued, and who or whatever is behind the message has my attention."

"Same here. What are you going to do?" his mom asked.

"I don't know. I need to shift and go for a run to think." Daniel set the empty beer bottle on the counter.

"Go and be careful."

Daniel went outside to his truck—the truck that used to be his dad's—pausing to run his hand along the dent in the driver's side door. He'd avoided bringing it into a shop to have the damage fixed. His mom thought it was morbid that he kept that reminder of the accident that took his dad's life, but it was a reminder for him that while his kind may have enhanced strength, reflexes, speed, and senses, they were mortal like humans. His dad's head had cracked against the window upon impact and broke open like an egg.

The door creaked on its hinges when he opened it. The truck was over ten years old now and had seen a lot of miles. He imagined his joints would be protesting like that someday, if he was fortunate enough to live a long life. He turned the key in the ignition, and the engine roared under the hood. Daniel pulled away from the curb and headed out beyond the city limits.

It hadn't been difficult to convince his mom to move back to Colorado. While West Virginia and Kentucky had some beautiful forests, they never felt connected to the East as they did with the wilderness of the Rockies. They had chosen Fort Collins since it backed to the Arapaho and Roosevelt National Forest. Acres of mountains and untamed land were a short drive away and offered plenty of space to discreetly shift and roam for hours. Away from the noise and distractions of civilization was where Daniel did his best thinking.

He found a deserted place to park in the shadows and climbed out. He raised his head, his nostrils flared as he scented the air, picking up all sorts of wild scents. His inner mountain lion itched to be free. *Soon*, he said to it and moved across the field toward the edge of the forest and the cover the tree line provided. Once there, he unlaced his boots and stripped off his clothes. His skin practically glowed in the moonlight, every muscle rippling with movement when he bent over to hide his clothes underneath a bush. He stayed in a crouch and called his animal forth. The familiar sting of claws breaking through the ends of his fingers and toes before his hands and feet transformed into paws came first. His bones snapped and muscles pulled as they made his new form. It was over in seconds, and then Daniel was loping through the woods, squirrels, birds, and rabbits scattering before him, ever wary of the predator that had just joined the night.

Dawn was approaching when he shifted back to his human form, his bones feeling heavy from exhaustion. Daniel slipped on his clothes and made his way back to his truck with purposeful strides. Listening to instinct, or whatever longing tugged at him from inside, he had made a decision. He was going to take a chance and call about the job in Havenwood Falls.

CHAPTER 3

"*P*arker's Perfect Placement Agency, this is Patty. How can I help you?" The woman who answered the phone had the chirpiest voice.

"Uh, hi, I'm calling about the construction foreman position."

"Oh, great, and how did you hear about this job?"

Daniel sat down at the table in the kitchen with the phone in his hand, a pencil in his other hand poised over a notepad. "A flyer was posted on the community board at Art's Variety in Fort Collins."

There was a pause, and all Daniel heard in the background was the *clack-clack* of keys on a typewriter. "Fort Collins. Wow, that's pretty far."

"Where exactly is Havenwood Falls?" Daniel asked. "I looked at a current map and couldn't find it anywhere."

"Well, that's because we're Colorado's best kept secret!" Daniel moved the phone away from his ear. The woman's voice was so sweet, he expected syrup to start pouring out of the receiver. "Now tell me your name. If you have the time, we can do a phone interview right now. The fact that you're calling because of the flyer pre-screened you."

"It did?" He thought that was strange, but he had never worked with an agency before, so he shrugged it off. "My name is Daniel McCabe."

Patty asked him about his construction background, of which he had plenty. He learned his trade from hands-on experience starting in high school. Once he graduated, he entered the industry full time, starting as a day laborer and working his way up. He provided three references and their phone numbers. Patty explained the job was for a new commercial building, but there were ample opportunities beyond that.

"Daniel, thank you for calling. I just need to call and check your references. Hopefully I'll have good news by the end of the day!" she chirped.

After the call disconnected, Daniel stared down at the notepad. His one question he had written down in advance remained unanswered: *Where is Havenwood Falls?*

Later that afternoon, Patty Parker called back and offered Daniel the job. They agreed that he would start the following Tuesday, but he needed to be there Monday to do paperwork. When he asked for directions, he was instructed to meet a shuttle bus in Grand Junction, and he could either take the shuttle or follow it into town.

"We're kind of in the middle of nowhere, and it's easy to get lost if you've never been here before," she explained.

DANIEL CLENCHED the steering wheel tight with anticipation as he drove past a sign constructed out of river rock, a blend of muted blues and grays. Black wrought iron lettering spelled out *Havenwood Falls*. His journey had been long, but uneventful. He took his time, keeping the shuttle in sight, but not taxing the old truck as the winding road climbed to higher elevations. With his windows down, the air was cool yet sweet from the lupines that lined the road, creating a colorful border for the dense forest that lay beyond. A hawk cried and circled in the sky ahead before disappearing in the tree tops. He sensed he was being watched. That something or someone was concealed in the woods, tracking his progress, and had been following him for a couple of miles, since he passed through an invisible border made of magic. It was subtle, a tickle across his skin, but magic nonetheless. He didn't sense a threat, so he had kept going.

Now the trees began to thin, and driveways appeared on the side of the road leading to small homes. Daniel continued on, following the shuttle, but he sensed he would have found his way on his own, if he focused on the internal tugging. It was like a magnetic attraction or an internal compass leading him in the right direction. The shuttle continued on the road that became Main Street. He drove past the high school, a three-story brick structure with arches marking the front entrance. A sign out front said "Congratulations to the Class of 1957! Go Dragons!"

Across the street, a restaurant was hopping. He spotted waitresses on roller skates expertly balancing trays full of food. He inhaled the aroma of grilled meat, and his stomach rumbled. Burger Bar was definitely going to be one of his first visits. There was a sign in the parking lot behind Burger Bar that said: "Miller's Plaza Coming Soon!" and he wondered if that was the project he would be involved with.

He continued on, and sun filtered through the trees that lined the street. He slowed down as he approached the shopping district, as there were a lot of pedestrians. People watched him drive by. Typical behavior for small towns, where the residents probably knew everyone and their vehicles. With the two-tone buttercream and brown paint job, plus the large dent in the driver's side, and the distinctive growl of the engine, his truck was one of a kind, and it was obvious, based on the stares, that they didn't recognize it.

He took note of Campbell's Market, the dark green canvas awning providing shade for fresh ears of corn, cucumbers, and tomatoes for sale in bins underneath a large window. He drove past a saloon and made note of that, too. The town square appeared to his left. A giant fountain in the middle sparkled in the sun. A jazz band was set up in the gazebo, playing to a small crowd. All of the buildings he saw were well maintained. He had entered a town worthy of a postcard.

As he drove through the center of Havenwood Falls, he became aware that not all of the people were human.

The shuttle parked along the curb in front of a gorgeous Victorian house, but Daniel kept going around the square. He pulled in next to a police cruiser when he parked in front of City Hall and caught the distinct odor of wolf. He turned in the direction of the scent and noticed the sheriff's deputy sitting in the cruiser, also scenting the air. Daniel hadn't gone undetected, either. The deputy narrowed his eyes, and they flashed a deep gold before returning to brown. Leaving his truck unlocked and windows down, figuring it was going to be searched anyway, Daniel left to find Parker's Perfect Placement Agency. According to the directions Patty gave him, it was located on Eleventh Street next to the bank, Havenwood Falls Savings & Loan.

A secretary sat behind a wide metal desk, typing away. Her fingers hitting the keys made a loud clacking noise. Her gray hair curled out at the ends and brushed the tops of her shoulders. She had a matronly look about her, and when she glanced up at Daniel, she pushed her tortoiseshell horn-rimmed glasses up her nose.

"Can I help you?" she asked in a no-nonsense tone, while still typing at a rapid-fire pace.

"Yes, my name is Daniel McCabe. I'm here to see Patty Parker." He handed her the flyer, and she gave it a brief glance before sighing and handing it back to him.

"Hold on, please." She stood and walked down a narrow hallway. There were two doors on the right and one on the left. She knocked on the door on the left before opening it and disappearing inside. She returned a moment later to bring Daniel back.

They stopped in front of a closed door. The bottom half was dark wood and the top half frosted glass, and etched in the glass in block letters was the name Martin Parker. A woman sat behind a cluttered desk. Her hair was brown and twisted up into a beehive. He showed her the flyer, and she grinned at him, her blue eyes sparkling behind her black-framed glasses.

"Mr. McCabe, pleased to meet you, finally. Patty Parker," she said and stood up to walk around the desk. She was taller than he expected and wore navy capri pants with a short jacket. "Please have a seat and pardon the mess. It's my husband's, and I'm attempting to organize."

Daniel took a seat in one of the two available chairs, and Patty handed him a clipboard with a bunch of forms. About fifteen minutes later, he was just finishing the last form when his nostrils flared. He scented the presence of a vampire—it had been a few years since he last encountered a vampire, but he'd recognize their scent of dusty blood anywhere—and two other creatures he wasn't familiar with. Suddenly the office door opened, and three people filed in: a tall older man with intense blue eyes and silvery blond hair that draped down to his lower back; the man next to him was the vampire, his grayish green eyes unlike any color Daniel had seen before; and the other man's scent was spicy, but his species eluded Daniel. What was going on? Everything about this situation was unusual, but things just kept getting more bizarre. His gut was telling him to proceed and that he wasn't in danger, so he decided to stay.

"You're a mountain lion shifter, correct?" the tall man with silvery hair asked.

"Yes. How did you know?" Daniel sat up straighter in his seat, taken aback at the man's directness.

"We have our ways, Mr. McCabe. I know you sensed we're not human, and there are others in town like us."

"Yes, I did."

"My name is Elsmed Fairchild, and I'll tell you, so you can stop guessing—I'm a fae. The vampire is Mihail Petran, and he owns Whisper Falls Inn. This other gentleman is Del Augustine, and he's a mage. Havenwood Falls isn't like other towns. Sure, there's the chamber of commerce, city hall, and city council, but the supernatural population requires a different structure and type of policing. That's where we come in. We sit on the Court of the Sun and the Moon and make sure everyone behaves in this town. If not, there are consequences." His blue eyes flared at this, driving his point home.

Daniel tapped his fingers against his leg, waiting for the other shoe to drop. So far everything had been going too smoothly.

"Relax, Daniel," Patty reassured him. "If we didn't think you'd be a good fit here, you wouldn't be sitting there."

"Exactly," Del said, his voice a soothing baritone. "The flyer you saw was spelled to only be seen by supernaturals."

"Oh, that makes sense. My mom said she smelled magic."

"Either she has a very keen nose, or I'm slipping," Patty said with a laugh that broke some of the tension in the room.

"The rules are simple, Daniel," Elsmed continued. "You can't show your shifter form or abilities in public, specifically in front of humans. This includes hunting. You also need to know that wards are in place that will alter your memory. If you leave Havenwood Falls, your memories of this town will fade until they're gone forever. Finally, you will be marked with a tattoo that identifies you as a supernatural and has certain magical qualities. For example, you'll have better control over your shift. We'll start you off with the temporary one and if you decide you like Havenwood Falls and want to live here long-term, we'll upgrade your tattoo. A permanent tattoo has benefits, such as being able to leave the wards for a full lunar cycle, or twenty-eight days, without your memories being affected. Any questions?"

"You want to tattoo me because I'm not human?" Daniel stood up, prepared to walk out. "Identifying a certain group by marking them is a tactic of war. I'm not comfortable with this." He crossed the room to the only window and peered out onto the side street. A mountain, one of the many peaks that surrounded Havenwood Falls, loomed above the neighborhoods behind the agency, and the evergreen tree line beckoned him, a promise of nocturnal romps within the forest. *Perhaps this town is too good to be true, after all*, he thought to himself.

"It's a temporary tattoo unless you choose to stay and make it permanent. It doesn't even have to be visible. It is a requirement if you plan to take the job and stay here." Del Augustine approached Daniel. He wore a three-piece suit, and gold cufflinks with the letter *A* inlaid with onyx stuck out from beneath the sleeves of his tailored jacket. Daniel tensed up when Del drew too close, and the mage backed off. "You don't trust easily, do you?" he asked Daniel.

"No."

"I understand, believe me. Our kind have been persecuted for centuries. Right, Patty?" Del called out across the room.

"We sure have. My ancestors fled Salem. Left in the dead of night before they could be accused."

"You see, all of us have been hunted or treated differently. Havenwood Falls was built as a safe haven for our kind. The rules we have are to ensure that safety isn't threatened."

As Del spoke, Daniel listened with all of his senses, and he didn't detect any type of deception. Taking a deep breath, he turned away from the window and faced the room.

"Fine. I'll agree to a tattoo, but it has to be invisible."

CHAPTER 4

*T*he sun was beginning to set when Daniel left PPP Agency. In his hands he had the keys to a cabin and the paperwork to start his new job the next day. His right shoulder blade itched. True to their word, his tattoo was invisible, but he still felt the tendrils of magic seeping into his skin. Still in shock and unsure what to make of his good fortune, he sat in his truck for a few minutes, letting everything sink in. First, he had to call his mom and let her know he'd made it to the town, and as his stomach growled, he realized had to find something to eat. Remembering the market he passed on the way in, he fired up the truck and backed out of the parking spot. Within minutes, he was pulling into a space along the curb right in front of Campbell's Market. A strange sensation, like his pulse beating along the surface of his skin, began when he stepped onto the sidewalk, and it grew stronger when he entered the store.

To the right was a single register and checkout counter, and next to it a stack of baskets. He grabbed one and made his way over to the refrigerated case along the back of the store, where all the meat was kept. Apparently, the cabin he was renting came fully furnished, including dishes and pots and pans. Daniel was used to his mom cooking for him, but he thought he could handle frying up a steak on the stove and making a potato. It couldn't be that difficult. Throwing a steak and a package of bacon in the basket, he made his way down the case and added a dozen eggs. As he walked down the canned goods aisle, the thrumming sensation on his skin increased in intensity, becoming more of a buzz, like he was on the receiving end of continuous low-level jolts of electricity. *What in the world?* he thought to himself, thinking it was the tattoo causing the sensation. And then he saw her, and he forgot about everything.

A young woman stood behind the register, ringing up a customer. Her hair was silken gold, and her skin the peaches and cream described in fairy tales. She reminded him of Grace Kelly, but he thought she was far more beautiful. She was the most gorgeous creature he had ever laid eyes on. The woman smiled at the customer, her full lips parting to reveal straight white teeth. Daniel stood frozen in the aisle, staring like an idiot. Even his inner beast had stilled, captivated by the tiny beauty.

Slowly he breathed in deeply through his nose. He filtered out extraneous odors, like the onions and peppers in the produce section and the bananas that were too ripe. Her perfume was a soft floral and so very feminine, but masked her true scent, and that was what Daniel was after. Buried underneath the perfume and soap was a scent that reminded him of sunshine and moonlight all at once. It called to him, and without realizing, he had taken a few steps forward, his body being pulled to her. Then his brain finally caught up with his senses when he fully processed what was unexpected about her scent.

She was human.

This fact stopped him cold, and he almost dropped the basket. Daniel was positive this woman was intended to be his mate. The visceral response to her left little doubt, but how could she be? He couldn't be with a human. That was an affront to his kind. As if he were standing next to him, his dad's voice echoed in his head. *"Humans are the predators, son. They seek out and destroy or try to control anyone they see as different."* Daniel knew this; history had proven it. So, with a heavy heart, he set the basket down and quickly left the market, ignoring the instinct that was urging him to claim the woman.

Sitting in his truck with the windows down, Daniel took several deep breaths in an attempt to clear his head, which was at war with his heart. The papers for his job and the keys to the cabin lay on the passenger seat. The promise of a life with some permanency was within reach, and he didn't realize how badly he wanted that until it was offered. The human woman complicated things.

A rap on the passenger door pulled Daniel from his thoughts. He turned his head to look at the older man who was bent over, elbows on the sill of the door, peering into the cab of the truck. He had deep wrinkles around his mouth and eyes, which were shrouded by wiry, bushy eyebrows that resembled steel wool. His gray hair was slicked back with pomade.

"Well, I'll be. You're the spitting image of him."

"Of who?"

"I wasn't sure, I mean McCabe is a common name, but when Elsmed told me you were a mountain lion shifter, I had to see for myself."

"What are you talking about and who are you?"

"Jerome Brewster. Are you heading to the cabin? I'll explain along the way." Daniel watched in disbelief as Jerome opened the door and climbed inside, sliding the paperwork and keys along the bench seat toward him. "Well, don't just sit there and stare at me catching flies. Drive. I'll give you directions, since you're new to town."

Shaking his head at the audacity of the strange old man, Daniel started the truck. He was curious who Jerome was and who Daniel reminded him of. Hoping the saying "curiosity killed the cat" didn't hold true, he pulled out onto Main Street and followed Jerome's instructions.

Once they were out of the downtown area, they followed the main road back out of town, until the sign showed it changing to County Road 13, although Jerome called it Burdorf Pass. When he turned right onto a dirt road, he recognized the cabins he had driven past on his way into town. Several log cabins were scattered among the trees, many partially hidden in shadows as the sun dipped behind the mountains to the west. He spotted cabin number four and pulled up in front of the single-story building. It was a simple structure with a window and a door on the front. A metal stovepipe rose from the roof.

Grabbing his suitcase from the bed of the truck, Daniel climbed up the three steps that led to the door and unlocked it. Pine-scented cleaner and wood polish assaulted his nose, and it took him a few minutes to adjust. Opening up a few windows to air the place out helped. On the counter there was a basket of cheese, sausage, crackers, and some apples as a welcome. Between that and the few sandwiches his mom had packed in a cooler for him, at least he had something to eat, since he left the market empty-handed.

The living room consisted of a love seat in the most god-awful pattern and a rocking chair.

"Have a seat." Daniel sat in the rocking chair, which creaked under his weight, and Jerome sunk down onto the loveseat, his equally creaky knees popping.

"Your grandfather saved my life," Jerome announced.

And the revelations kept coming. Daniel was surprised he wasn't dizzy from all the information being dumped on him. First the supernatural secret society of Havenwood Falls and now this. "What?"

"I was at Sunset Creek that night everything went to shit. You do know about Sunset Creek, don't you, son?"

Daniel nodded. "Yes, my dad told me—he even brought me there."

Jerome shook his head and frowned. The wrinkles around his mouth deepened. "I know Ian got his wife and son out. Then he came back to help others escape. I was the last one he saved. As I was running with my son in my arms and my wife running alongside me, I briefly looked back over my shoulder just as a burning building collapsed. It was like a wave of fire washed over your granddad. Only a fire dragon could have survived that."

"Wow." That's all Daniel could say. After seeing the decades-old ruins in Sunset Creek when he was a teen, it was easy to imagine his grandfather's painful death.

"What are the odds that you show up here," Jerome said and rose to his feet with a groan. "I can't pay your grandfather back for saving me, but I can return the favor to you. Anything you need, boy, don't hesitate to ask. My family has a cabin just around the bend—number 9."

"Thank you." Daniel shook his hand and watched as the old man sauntered down the driveway.

"What are the odds, indeed?" Daniel muttered under his breath.

CHAPTER 5

One minute the handsome stranger was standing in the aisle, resembling a deer trapped in headlights as he stared at her, and the next minute he was gone. He had set his full basket down on the floor and bolted out the door like his Levi's were on fire. Before Colleen could call after him, the door had swung shut.

Maybe he forgot his wallet, she thought to herself, and shook her head. That wasn't the first strange thing to have happened in town, and surely wouldn't be the last. She did wonder about the man. He wasn't from around here, for she would have heard about him from her girlfriends. A man that looked like he did would not escape their attention. He was tall, muscular, and had the most incredible blue eyes that were accentuated by his dark eyebrows. His reddish-brown hair was thick on top and had a slight pompadour. Sideburns added to the definition of his sharp cheekbones. If she hadn't been busy ringing up a customer, she probably would have been caught up in his intense gaze. Sighing, she smoothed the apron she wore over her Madrid print capri pants and salmon-colored blouse, before retrieving the stranger's basket and putting back the items, taking note of the toiletry items and the thick steak swimming in blood.

Perhaps he was a tourist passing through Havenwood Falls, here to take advantage of the hiking and fishing. Maybe he was visiting family.

Colleen hoped he came back, so she could at least learn a name to go with the handsome face. She grinned at the memory of doodling her name in her school notebooks and adding the last name of whoever she had crushed on at the time. Sadly, none of those crushes had panned out. Some turned out to be jerks, and others left Havenwood Falls after graduation and never returned. Now some of her friends were beginning to settle down. At twenty years old, she was already past the age her mom was when her parents were married. So far, Colleen hadn't found anyone even remotely close to husband material, and in the small town, her chances of finding someone were slim.

She shook her head and scoffed at the direction her thoughts had taken. Just one glimpse of the handsome stranger and she was already thinking marriage. Perhaps planning her friend Peggy's bridal shower was responsible.

The small bell above the front door to the store chimed, and Colleen looked up from where she was dusting and straightening the rows of canned vegetables. Her dad walked in, carrying a wooden box with the Stone Falls Winery logo burned into the side.

"Howdy, pumpkin!" he called and set the box down next to the register. The bottles inside rattled slightly with the movement.

"Hi, Daddy!" Colleen said and walked over to meet him.

"The Blackstones gave me a great deal on this case of cabernet." He pulled out a bottle and held it up to the light. "I can't wait to bring this home for your mother. Her bridge club will love it."

He winked at her and set the bottle back in the crate. While he went to the back of the store, where his office was located, Colleen counted down the register and started closing everything down for the night. The sun had set, and the dinner rush was over. At seven o'clock on the nose, she locked the door and flipped the sign from *Open* to *Closed*.

Together they walked out to the street where her parents' station wagon was parked. Her dad was quite proud of the fact that they had the only wagon in town with the wood paneling on the sides. The drive home only took about five minutes. They lived at the end of Fairchild Lane where it dead-ended. Their house backed up to Bels

Creek, which Colleen could actually see through the trees when she looked out her bedroom window.

Instead of going to college or moving to a big city after she graduated high school, Colleen had stayed home and taken on more responsibilities at her family's business. She had recently become the assistant manager, and she was salting her wages away into a nest egg for when she did move out on her own or got married.

As if reading her mind, her dad broke the silence inside the car. "Pumpkin, I appreciate you taking on the assistant manager position. It's nice knowing I can leave to run errands and know the store is in good hands."

"Aw, Daddy, thank you." She leaned over and pecked him on the cheek, which crinkled when he immediately smiled.

"I know it won't be long before someone comes along and sweeps you off your feet, then you'll kick your old man to the curb."

Colleen shook her head, causing her blond hair to bounce. "I don't think that will happen anytime soon," she protested, but immediately thought of the mysterious man who had run out of the store earlier. A vision flashed of her holding his hand while her free hand rested on her belly, swollen with child. A gasp escaped her lips and snapped her out of the daydream. She was surprised to find she was holding her stomach, like in her vision.

"Are you okay, pumpkin?" Her dad's brown eyes were full of concern when he turned to look at her.

"Yes, I'm fine," Colleen said and quickly moved her hand onto her lap.

Before her father could say anything else, they had arrived at home, and he was pulling into the driveway. The azaleas and rhododendron in the front flower beds were in full bloom. Some of the blossoms reached as high as the porch railing. The Campbells lived in a Victorian painted a light lavender with darker purple trim. The garage used to be a carriage house, back when horses were the main mode of transportation. It was just large enough to accommodate the station wagon. Her dad didn't pull into the carriage house, though, and before he turned off the engine, Colleen ran on ahead inside, leaving her dad to get the sack of groceries. The screen door slammed shut behind her, and she slipped off her white Keds before running up the stairs to her right.

Once in her room with the door shut, she took a few deep breaths to collect herself. That vision had felt so real, like she was really pregnant, and as she ran a hand over her flat stomach, she actually mourned for the child that never existed. *What on earth?* she asked herself, bewildered at the range of emotions.

After running a brush through her hair, pulling it up in a ponytail, and tying it with a ribbon that matched her shirt, Colleen went back downstairs to join her family for dinner. They were already in the dining room. Her dad was seated at the end of the table with his back to a window that looked out over the side yard. Her seventeen-year-old sister, Kelly, and her fourteen-year-old brother, David, were seated to his left. Colleen's mom was just setting the platter containing a roast on the table right next to a vase displaying a gorgeous arrangement of fresh flowers. Colleen sat down to the right of her dad and her mom took the seat at the other end of the table. They joined hands and said grace before diving in. Bowls and platters were passed around until everyone had full plates. David's practically spilled over onto the lace tablecloth.

"Ellen, you outdid yourself with this fine feast," her father praised, and Colleen grinned when her mom blushed from the compliment. Forks scraped against porcelain as they ate and chatted about their days. Callum presented a bottle of cabernet from the crate, and Colleen's mom opened it, filling the wine glasses for her and her husband, as well as Colleen.

"So, David, what did you do today?" Callum asked.

"Oh, my day was real swell, Dad! I spent the day on Mathews River with Billy and Dewey. We went fishing and swimming."

"Did you catch anything?"

"No. Well, Dewey hooked an old boot, but that's it. Oh, and we saw a giant wolf. Billy claims he saw its eyes glow, but I didn't see anything like that." David's face lit up as he recounted his adventure.

"Callum, this is why I get nervous with David running around all day. What if he had been attacked? Lord knows what else is in the woods."

Colleen finished taking a sip of wine before chiming in. "The animals were here first. We're encroaching on their land. It's only natural they're going to be seen by the river. It's one of the few water sources around here. Imagine how they feel. We've moved in and taken over, just like with the Indians."

The room grew quiet, and Colleen looked around the table. Her mom's lips were a straight line, her eyes narrowed in disapproval. "Being vocal about such controversial viewpoints won't win you any suitors, Colleen," she said.

"Well, I'd prefer a suitor who shares my views and doesn't mind a woman who speaks her mind."

Kelly snorted, and Colleen turned to look at her sister. She had clamped a hand over her mouth, but it didn't cover up the grin she was trying to conceal. They both had opinions about being stuck at home to be housewives and spent many nights sneaking into one another's bedrooms to discuss their dreams of changing the world. For Colleen, she saw how the town was creeping farther and farther into the wilderness that surrounded them. She wanted to protect the animals and their habitat. Kelly wanted to break barriers and become the first female fighter pilot in the Air Force. Watching films about the daredevil heroes who flew bombers during World War II had left quite a lasting impression on her sister.

"Callum, say something," Ellen pleaded, but he only winked, his brown eyes twinkling with amusement.

"I agree with Colleen. I want both my girls to find men worthy of them and their passions. Just like you, Ellen. It wasn't so long ago when you were coordinating letter-writing efforts for our troops and supporting the young wives left behind."

"Not me. I'm never getting married. I'm going to stay here forever," David announced, before stuffing a piece of roast beef in his mouth. "Mom's cooking is too good to leave behind." This statement was muffled as he chewed and spoke at the same time. Ellen gave him a pointed look in reprimand at his poor manners but couldn't help but laugh at his declaration. This dissolved any tension in the room.

Later that night, Colleen tossed and turned, her dreams invaded by the stranger from the store. His blue eyes as his gaze traveled the length of her body, warming her from the inside out. She could even smell him in her dreams, and when she woke up, the scent lingered. A mix of balsam and something spicy. Blaming it on the open bedroom windows and the smell of the forest being carried in on the slight breeze, Colleen got up to close the window closest to her bed.

The moon was full and illuminated everything in a silvery light. Looking out into the backyard, she almost missed the animal partially shrouded in shadow, until it moved. The movement caused the creature's eyes to glimmer in the moonlight. Colleen gasped and took a step backward, even though she was on the third floor and safe inside the house. Once over the initial shock, she returned to the window and leaned forward, her elbows on the sill. After a few minutes, the animal stepped out of the shadows to reveal a gorgeous mountain lion. Muscles rippled beneath its fur coat as it moved. Then it sat down on its haunches and raised its gaze to meet Colleen's.

She wasn't sure how long they stared at each other, but she was captivated by the odd interaction, which was interrupted by a yawn. Her skin was chilled by the night air, and she shivered. When she stood upright, the mountain lion got up, too. She raised her arm and waved farewell. Colleen watched as the giant cat slipped in between the trees that grew along the edge of the yard and disappeared, before turning away and climbing into bed, burrowing under the covers.

The next morning, she woke and stretched, not feeling completely rested because of all the vivid dreams. When she walked past the window, she paused and looked outside for any sign of a mountain lion. The only wildlife in the backyard was a squirrel. The light of day gave her a new perspective on the previous night's events. *It was just a dream*, she convinced herself, and continued on with getting ready for work.

CHAPTER 6

*W*ith a groan, Daniel sat up, swinging his legs over the side of his bed. He was buck naked, and shredded bits of clothes were strewn all over the hardwood floor in the cabin. Streaks of mud stained the bright white sheets, and pine needles fell from his hair when he ran his hand through it.

"Damn it," he muttered under his breath and stood up, stretching out his body.

Between the full moon and the lure of his mate being so close, he was unable to resist shifting and seeking her out. While he thought he may come to regret his actions later, he enjoyed observing his mate at her home. When she appeared in the window, he practically froze. Her blond hair was rumpled from sleep, and he saw the outline of her curves through the fabric of her nightgown. With his keen eyesight, he noticed when her nipples hardened right when she saw him. She was like Rapunzel in her tower, and everything about her called to him. It took every ounce of control to stay in one spot when all he had wanted to do was scale the wood siding of her house to reach her. Fortunately, he hadn't done anything that would make her think he was anything but an ordinary mountain lion.

It was his first night in Havenwood Falls, and he had already showed himself to a human. When he met with Elsmed Fairchild the day before, the fae had explained how the town came to be. That the founding families were made of various supernatural species, from werewolves—including the town's sheriff, Ric Kasun—to vampires, witches, fae, and more. They were all seeking a safe haven and found it in the picturesque box canyon. The surrounding mountains provided a natural barrier, but wards and spells provided a magical boundary for additional protection. The humans who lived in town, with the exception of a few, like the town mayor, didn't know that supernaturals existed, and the Court—the supernatural governing body made up of members of the founding families—wanted to keep the humans as uninformed as possible. That meant not doing anything supernatural in front of them. At least he hadn't shifted in public. Only a mountain lion would have been seen roaming through town, if there were any other witnesses, which he hoped there weren't. He was lucky he didn't get shot. His new beginning was off to a stellar start.

Crossing the bedroom to the tiny bathroom, Daniel peered in the mirror at the stubble that had sprouted up overnight. After shaving, making sure to shape his sideburns, he showered, removing all evidence of his nocturnal romp.

The parking lot at Burger Bar was deserted when he drove past to reach the jobsite. A Silverstream trailer was set up in the packed down dirt directly behind the restaurant. He parked next to it and got out of his truck. Daniel had been told to report at seven o'clock, and had arrived a few minutes early on purpose. He wanted to get a feel for the landscape and scope of the project. The ground had been broken during a big ceremony with the mayor cutting a ribbon and everything, but after that, Miller's Plaza had stalled because of labor issues. Apparently, Ross Builders had been experiencing a string of bad luck in keeping people employed. The last foreman had disappeared overnight. This was why the owner, Herschel Ross, had started recruiting in other parts of the state.

Miller's Plaza was a big commercial initiative that would create more retail and office space beyond the town square. An excavator was parked off to the side near a flatbed trailer stacked with steel beams. Patty told him the day before that Herschel had said the city was ready to run sewer and water lines once the holes were dug. That would be step one. Then they'd dig a hole and pour the basement. From there, the buildings would go up fairly quickly.

Daniel leaned against his truck and poured some hot coffee from his Thermos while he waited for Herschel and the rest of the crew to show up. He was anxious to take a look at the blueprints. From where he stood, he had a good view of Main Street. Traffic was light, but he imagined once school was back in session, it would be busier.

A pale green International pickup truck turned into the entrance and came to a stop next to Daniel's truck. "Ross Builders" was written on the side with dark blue paint. An older man stepped out. He wore faded dungarees and a dark green Western-style shirt. The buttons looked strained as the shirt stretched across a rotund belly.

"You must be Daniel McCabe," he said and extended his hand. "I'm Herschel Ross."

"Nice to meet you, sir." Daniel shook Herschel's hand. He had a strong grip and plenty of calluses. Those came with the trade.

"Well, Patty Parker from the temp agency spoke very highly of you. Are you ready to get to work?"

"Yes, sir."

Daniel followed Herschel into the Airstream trailer, which served as the jobsite office. The dinette area on the right, with the built-in table, served as the desk. Blueprints, invoices, and newspapers were scattered everywhere. The sink and counter in the kitchen area to the left were spilling over with dirty dishes. Several grease-stained waxed paper wrappers with the Burger Bar logo were on the floor. Cigar smoke permeated the air, making Daniel want to stop breathing. He imagined if Herschel went camping, he'd leave his garbage behind in the forest. Another reason he disliked humans—they didn't appreciate the environment.

"Have a seat. We'll go over the plans."

Daniel shoved some papers aside and sat down on the bench. Herschel dug through the pile and pulled out a roll of blueprints. He unrolled them across the top of everything. There were so many lumps pushing up from underneath, it resembled more of a topographic map.

They spent close to thirty minutes going over the plans and schedule. When the rest of the crew arrived, Herschel introduced Daniel. The crew was small, and half of the eight men looked like they were approaching retirement age. One of the crew members, a tall man with olive skin and dark hair named Mickey, shook Daniel's hand. As he did, a gust of wind blew, and Daniel caught his scent. Mickey wasn't human either. A subtle nod passed between them, an acknowledgment that they both recognized each other's supernatural side.

As the day progressed, the cool morning burned away under a cloudless sky. The sun beat down on the crew as they worked. Daniel paused to wipe sweat from his brow and take a drink of water from the canteen he brought. The water was no longer cool, but it was wet and kept him from dehydrating. He took off his shirt and tossed it onto the seat of his truck through the open window. When he leaned back against the hood, enjoying a hint of breeze, he stared up at Main Street. Traffic had picked up, and Burger Bar was hopping. Waitresses wearing pink dresses with white aprons, notepads hanging out of their front pockets, whizzed through the parking lot deftly, carrying trays loaded with burgers, fries, and shakes. They navigated around cars and people with the grace of dancers and were a mesmerizing sight. The smell of grilled meat and fried food made his stomach growl, and the sandwich in his lunchbox was suddenly unappealing.

At high noon, Herschel came out of the job trailer and sent everybody to lunch.

"Be back in an hour—sharp!" he yelled before disappearing back inside.

Daniel shook his head. No wonder Herschel had a hard time keeping people. His management style was awful. Daniel had seen his type before, the kind who hired people to do the dirty work while they stayed clean and barked orders. Daniel preferred to work alongside his crew. Not only did it help to earn their respect, but working hard made the day go by fast.

Reaching into his truck, Daniel grabbed his shirt and lunchbox. He walked past Burger Bar and made a right on Main Street.

He remembered seeing some benches in the town square and found an empty one underneath a large oak tree and completely covered in shade. Daniel sat down with a groan. His shoulders and back were already tight from the morning spent shoveling and moving dirt. It was at least ten degrees cooler in the shade, and he took a moment to close his eyes and lean his head back. His roaming the night before had cut into his sleep. Between being tired and his sore muscles, he felt like an old man. The scrape of his lunchbox sliding toward him on the bench and the most irresistible scent caused him to open his eyes and sit up with a jerk. There, sitting next to him, was the woman from the market. She had a paper bag on her lap and was looking at him with deep brown eyes. A shy smile lifted her pink lips.

"I hope you don't mind. There's room for two." She gestured at the respectable distance between them.

"Uh, no, you're fine," Daniel responded stiffly and popped the latch open on his lunchbox, hoping the distraction of food would help him to ignore the woman. Now that she was sitting right next to him, his senses were overwhelmed. His whole body coiled tight—even his toes in his work boots were curled. He needed to keep from making a scene. He wanted to pounce on her, touch her, rub against her, bite her, and mark her. He'd be hauled away in a second. The police station was within eyesight.

Out of the corner of his eye, Daniel saw her pull out a book from the bag, and she opened it up on her lap. She held a sandwich in one hand, taking dainty bites whenever she turned the page. Her blond hair was just long enough to brush the tops of her shoulders and curl up at the ends, and her bangs curled down over her forehead. She had an adorable nose that turned up slightly at the end. A bread crumb clung to the corner of her mouth, and he became fixated on it. How that crumb teased him. All he had to do was lean over and lick it off, but one taste would lead him down a rabbit hole, and he'd be lost in his own Wonderland and simply mad.

"Aren't you hungry?" Her soft voice broke through his haze. He forced himself to look away from the taunting crumb and meet her eyes. She was blushing and chewing on her bottom lip like she was trying to stop from laughing.

"What?" He felt disoriented, like the first time he got drunk on whiskey. It was right after he had watched his dad get lowered into the damp ground. He remembered staring at the dirt under his fingernails as he held a tumbler in his hand. Dirt from the handful he had tossed on top of the casket. He sat at the bar in a room full of strangers, isolated by his grief and his lack of close relationships. Daniel's dad had been his rock. They had moved so much that faces, except for his family's, became a blur. Now he looked at this woman, and her face was so clear, while everything else was blurry.

"You haven't touched your lunch." She pointed at his lunchbox. He had gotten as far as opening the darn thing but had been too busy staring at the human woman, making a fool of himself.

"Oh, I guess not." He ran a hand through his hair and looked away. Daniel didn't embarrass easily, but this woman had him all out of sorts. Then he glanced at his wristwatch and cursed. He had five minutes to get back to the job site. He mumbled an apology and grabbed his stuff.

A faint giggle followed him as he rushed off.

"I'll be here again tomorrow, same time!" she called after him.

Her invitation caused him to slow down. He spun so he walked backwards, wanting one last glance at his fair-haired temptress. That's exactly what she was, a temptress. Why would fate be so cruel as to make his mate a human? Committing his final glance to memory—the way her hair blew in the gentle breeze and how her brown eyes lit up when she smiled, which revealed a dimple. And she was smiling, smiling at him. His inner cat growled when Daniel turned away and ran through the square, his lunchbox knocking against his leg. By the time he crossed Fourth Street, he slowed down and walked the rest of the way. When he reached the jobsite, it wasn't just his inner beast growling, but his stomach. He'd just have to eat lunch in his truck from now on.

∽

THAT VERY NIGHT, he found himself in the woman's backyard. He paced in the shadows, his paws barely making a sound, muffled by soft earth and grass. Clouds had moved in, rendering the dark an extra inky black and lending a stillness to the damp air. The dampness amplified the scent of everything. The sweetness of roses blooming and the aroma of rosemary in the herb garden were strong scents, but not strong enough to cover up that of his mate. He'd recognize her anywhere.

All of the windows in the house were dark. The occupants had been asleep for hours. Daniel had watched as an older woman, who bore a strong resemblance to his mate, washed dishes before turning off the light. A young boy in a bedroom on the second floor had been playing a record, and the twang of Johnny Cash could be heard through the open window, but he eventually settled down. Anytime there was movement in his mate's window, his eyes were immediately drawn to it. When he was at just the right angle, he saw her at a vanity, brushing her hair. He longed to run his fingers through those silky strands. She, too, went to bed, and yet Daniel stayed, unable to pull himself away.

When the sky began to lighten to the east, he reluctantly stepped into the thatch of trees and ran along the river, following its curve through the forest until he crossed County Road, reaching his cabin, where he fell into bed.

Managing a little less than three hours of sleep, Daniel arrived at the jobsite looking as refreshed as a hungover hobo, or his boss. Herschel rolled out of the job trailer wearing the same sweat-stained clothes as the day before, and reeking of beer. He squinted his bloodshot eyes and peered out at the crew, which had decreased by one. After barking out orders and announcing the foundation would be poured that afternoon, Herschel disappeared back inside his trailer, leaving Daniel to manage the day's work, not that he minded. The group of six sweaty men smelled better than his boss.

When lunchtime rolled around, Herschel didn't make an appearance, so Daniel dismissed the workers. Mickey, the shifter, asked if he wanted to go to Burger Bar. At first, he was going to say yes, because he wasn't going back to the square and back to that bench, but ten minutes later, Daniel found himself in the same spot, waiting for his temptress to arrive.

He saw her when she emerged from underneath the shade of the awning in front of Campbell's Market. She waited for a 56 Merc to drive by before crossing Eighth Street. When she looked up and saw Daniel sitting on the bench, she flashed a wide smile and waved. She was wearing a pair of navy-and-white-striped capris, white Keds, and a white shirt. She skipped over and sat down next to him.

"I'm Colleen, by the way." She held out her hand, and Daniel grinned at her forwardness.

"Daniel," he said and shook her hand. The moment they touched, he knew he was doomed. It was like his pulse jumped to meet hers. Her brown eyes, which were framed by the longest, thickest lashes, widened, and she gasped. This was how he knew she felt the connection, too.

They stayed like that for a few moments, hands and eyes locked on each other. Only when two teenage girls walked by giggling did they separate. Colleen blushed, her fair skin flaring a beautiful dusty pink. Reaching for her lunch bag, she pulled out a sandwich along with a bottle of Coca-Cola, followed by a hardcover book. This time, Daniel glanced at the cover. She was reading *Peyton Place*, one of the previous year's best sellers. He heard it was being made into a movie.

Actually eating his lunch this time, Daniel ate his sandwich and took time to observe the town. Here in the square, he was basically sitting in the heart of Havenwood Falls. Whisper Falls Inn, a beautifully restored Victorian, sat kitty-corner. Baskets of purple and pink petunias were hanging along the eaves of the front porch. The bank, located next to PPP Agency, had a steady stream of people coming and going. He could see two ladies in the window of the beauty parlor sitting in chairs with their heads underneath some sci-fi-looking contraption.

"You're not from around here, are you?" Colleen asked out of the blue. Turning to look at her, he saw her book was closed on the bench between them. She had finished her lunch and had moved so she sat at an angle, facing him. Her legs were crossed at the ankle and her left arm was draped over the top of the back of the bench, her fingers inches from his face. This position caused the buttons on her blouse to gap slightly, and he caught a glimpse of her white bra.

Swallowing hard and tearing his gaze away from her breasts, he met her eyes. "No, I'm not. This is my first week here."

"I thought so. Everyone basically knows everyone in Havenwood Falls."

"Have you lived here long?"

"Born and raised." She stared wistfully off toward Mount Alexa. The peaks were still capped with snow even though summer was already underway. "I've never really been anywhere else. Where are you from?" she asked, turning her attention back to him.

Daniel sighed and stretched his legs out before him, settling in to the conversation. "All over really. My family moved around a lot. I'm from Colorado originally, though, and just moved back after spending ten years in Kentucky and West Virginia."

"Golly! What was that like?"

"Different, but the same. People don't really change, just the landscape."

"Huh." Colleen contemplated his statement. "I never really thought about it that way." She moved her arm from the back of the bench and started gathering her things together. Tucking her hair behind her ear, she stood up. "I have to get back to work and I'm off tomorrow, so maybe I'll see you Friday?"

"Maybe."

Her smile faded slightly at his noncommittal response. "I understand. It was nice meeting you, Daniel."

With a final wave, she rushed off in the direction of the market. He watched her until she was safely across the street and inside. The moment she was gone from sight, a small ache formed in his chest, like a mild case of heartburn, but not quite. Frowning, he rubbed at it and kept rubbing at his chest as he walked back to the jobsite. It grew increasingly worse as the day progressed.

"You look like you need a drink," Mickey said as he helped Daniel clean up at the end of the day. The concrete had been poured, and there wasn't much else they could do until it cured enough. That meant they had the next day off.

Hoping a drink would take the edge off the burning sensation, Daniel agreed. Half an hour later, they were parked on two bar stools at the Haven Saloon. As soon as they were seated, Mickey ordered them each a shot of whiskey and a mug of Coors beer.

The whiskey had an interesting golden glow to it, and Daniel's inner lion became piqued with interest, making him realize this wasn't ordinary hooch. He lifted the shot glass and raised an eyebrow at Mickey.

"Apparently there's a secret ingredient. Warded Whiskey, the Tinker's Drink, has been distilled right here in Havenwood Falls since the 1800s. There was a couple who owned a shop right on the square, and they made clocks, puzzle boxes, all sorts of early engineering type gadgets. The guy, Gregory, built a still, and it took off from there."

Mickey raised his glass, and they both tipped the whiskey back with one swallow. Daniel coughed, and his eyes watered as the liquor burned a path down his esophagus. Once the liquid hit his stomach, warmth bloomed from within, like a mushroom cloud had erupted from his core. His already acute eyesight sharpened, and his other senses became more heightened so suddenly, the saloon, which was already loud, became almost painful to his ears. Chasing the whiskey with a gulp of Coors was like dousing flames with water, and his body returned to normal except for the looseness of his muscles, which usually took a six-pack to achieve.

"Holy Toledo, that is some potent juice!" He wiped his mouth with the back of his hand and noticed his lips were slightly numb, like he had been out in the cold too long.

"One of Havenwood Falls' best kept secrets," Mickey said with a wink.

"What's yours?" Daniel asked, keeping his voice low. "I know you're a shifter. I just can't tell what kind."

"Hawk. And you're some kind of big cat, am I right?"

Daniel nodded and took another swallow of beer. "Mountain lion."

"In the normal animal kingdom, we wouldn't be getting along like this. Cats and birds don't mix well," Mickey said with a grin and waved the bartender over for another round. "How are you at darts?"

Turned out, with their preternatural eyesight, they became competitive and kept playing to one up the other. Five rounds of drinks and five games later, they stumbled out the door into a town transformed by dusk. This was Daniel's first time in town during the evening as a human, and he stopped in his tracks to take in the soft glow from gas-lit street lamps. They cast a flickering light on the sidewalk and sides of buildings. Garlic and other spices laced the cool air, and his stomach growled.

"I'm famished, too. Been to Napoli's yet?" Mickey asked, and Daniel shook his head. "Come on. Their food is cheap and tasty."

Daniel fell into step alongside Mickey, their strides evenly matched. Mickey was about Daniel's height, which put him around six feet tall. They crossed Main Street and walked down Eighth Street on the storefront side. Daniel paused outside Campbell's Market and raised his head, scenting the air and inhaling the faint traces of Colleen that seemed to permeate the building. The store was closed, and all of the lights were off except for those of the cooler that ran along the back wall. Bottles of milk and blocks of cheese and butter lined the shelves.

"Hey, blockhead." Mickey tapped Daniel's shoulder, getting his attention. "They're closed. Food is this way."

Backwoods Sport & Ski was still open. The front window displays featured mannequins dressed in the latest summer hiking and fishing gear. A wooden canoe filled the whole length of one of the two windows. Daniel made a note to stop in and replace the Levi's he destroyed in his uncontrolled shift the other night. The scent of garlic grew stronger as they made a left on Stuart Street. The fire department, a two-story brick building with two arched garage bays, was all lit up. One of the garage doors was open, revealing a shiny red firetruck. A Dalmatian lay in front, watching the street with alert eyes. It was a scene straight out of a Norman Rockwell painting until the dog turned its head toward them and growled slightly, most likely sensing the animals lurking beneath their skin.

Napoli's was a small restaurant around the corner from the town square. A screen door let out the noise of several conversations as well as the tantalizing smell of food. A teenage girl greeted them when they walked in. She wore a black poodle skirt and a white shirt. Her brown hair was pulled back in a ponytail tied with a red ribbon.

"Welcome to Napoli's!" she chirped, greeting them with a bright smile and more enthusiasm than an entire glee club. She grabbed two menus, and they followed her down a narrow aisle between tables, her wide skirt brushing against chairs and patrons as she charged ahead. There was something about the girl that seemed familiar to Daniel, but he knew he hadn't met her before.

They were seated at a booth in the back near the kitchen. Minutes later, a woman closer to their age came to take their orders. She introduced herself as Karine. She had thick dark hair, the tight curls pinned close to her head, and large green eyes that were accentuated by thick, contoured eyebrows. Daniel was briefly distracted by her red lips before noticing the apron tied at her waist showed off her curves. She could have easily been one of those girls painted on WWII fighter jets. He realized the normal attraction he should have experienced wasn't there. This woman paled in comparison to Colleen. *Geezum crow*, three days around her and she was deep under his skin. The bird taking their order didn't do anything for him. All he wanted, all his inner mountain lion wanted, was Colleen. A human.

Suddenly, his buzz dissipated, and after the waitress left, he let out an exasperated sigh and leaned back heavily in the booth.

"What's eating you?" Mickey asked, before taking a sip of Coca-Cola through a straw.

Daniel surveyed his new friend. Mickey was a shifter, and by the looks of him, an Indian. Out of anyone, he had to understand.

Leaning forward in his seat, he gestured for Mickey to lean forward too, so other diners in the cramped restaurant didn't overhear.

"I met my mate. She's here in Havenwood Falls."

"That's fantastic, daddy-o! Why do you seem so gloomy about it?"

"She's—" Daniel paused. "She's human," he whispered.

Mickey's face transformed from a smile to a scowl, and he moved away. He tapped his fingers on the table and regarded Daniel.

"Are you a purist?" he finally asked.

"A what?"

"A purist. You only procreate within your own kind and shun everything else. You didn't strike me as one, but if you have an issue with your own mate—which is a gift not to be spurned—because she's human, then I guess I was wrong about you." Mickey made a move to leave, a look of disgust on his face.

"Hold on," Daniel said. "Let me explain."

At that moment, Karine returned with their food. They had each ordered a large pizza and an order of garlic knots. As soon as they were alone and in between mouthfuls of food, Daniel told Mickey about Sunset Creek and how that history was behind every move his family had made.

"That's how I was raised. That's all I know, but Colleen—she's mine. I can feel it here." Daniel pounded on his chest above his heart. "How can she be my mate? It doesn't make sense."

Mickey set his slice of pizza down. "My ancestors helped to build this town alongside the founding families. All of the founders were either hunted or cast out because of their supernatural abilities. Witches and witch hunters helped to build Havenwood Falls— together. My great-great-grandmother was a white woman and a witch. My great-great-grandfather is from the Chickasaw tribe. Their relationship was forbidden by society, yet they found a way. You can figure this out. But to deny your mate? You know what that means, right?"

Daniel nodded and looked away from Mickey's intense dark gaze. He knew what it meant, and as the whiskey wore off, the physical effects were no longer masked. The ache was back.

After eating, they walked back to the jobsite where Daniel had left his truck, but as they passed Burger Bar, which sat dark and quiet, Daniel caught the scent of blood in the air. He raised his head slightly and inhaled deeply through his nose. It had the distinct smell of humans. Animal blood had a richness to it that human blood lacked. Mickey came to a stop, his head tilted to the side and his eyes closed. Suddenly his eyes popped open, and he started running toward the jobsite. Daniel immediately followed, not wanting his friend to go into an unknown situation alone. He could see at night almost as well as during the day. A man was laying on the ground, moaning.

They each came to a stop on either side of the man, whose face was beaten to a pulp. Daniel almost didn't recognize Herschel, if it wasn't for the clothes. They were stained with sweat earlier, and now they were soaked with blood. Alcohol wafted off his body like he had been soaking in a vat of whiskey.

"Mr. Ross, can you hear me?" Mickey asked. He rolled Herschel onto his back, and the man let out a hoarse cry that tapered off to a whimper.

"Christ, he's a mess," Daniel said, noting the crushed nose and eyes swollen shut. Herschel tried to say something, but his jaw hung at an angle, making it impossible for him to produce words. Drool, tinged pink from blood, dribbled down the side of his mouth. "Help me lift him up. He needs a doctor."

Herschel cried out when they lifted him off the ground. Mickey was at his feet, and Daniel supported the almost unconscious man with his hands hooked underneath his arms. Together they carried him up the slight incline to Main Street and the short distance to the medical center, which looked more like a house from the outside, not a hospital.

There was one nurse on duty, and she came running from the reception desk when she saw them outside the front door. She held it open so they could carry Herschel inside. He had passed out during the brief walk. Daniel noticed her nametag pinned to her starched white dress uniform when he passed by: Sharon Heller, RN.

"What happened?" she asked as they followed her down a short hallway, austere and sterile in its white brilliance.

"We found him like that," Daniel answered. "But I don't think he got this way from falling down the stairs."

Mickey snorted and almost dropped Herschel's feet. The jostling woke him up, and he started to thrash.

"Getoffme!" His swollen lips and lopsided jaw garbled his words.

"Herschel, knock it off!" Nurse Heller commanded, causing Daniel and even Mickey to stand up straight. "These fine young men are trying to help you." She continued to chastise him after they had set him down on a gurney.

"You know him?" Daniel asked.

Nurse Heller looked up at him, the stethoscope still stuck in her ears. "We grew up together, and he's always been a grump. It's a chronic ailment," she said with a wink before shooing them out of the cramped exam area.

A small waiting area, to the right of the main entrance, was where they wound up. Several wooden benches, which reminded Daniel of church pews with their straight backs, lined the walls. He leaned his head back against the cool plaster and stretched his legs out in front of him. Dust coated the tops of his boots. Mickey sat down next to him. He leaned forward with his elbows on top of his knees. His head hung down, almost like he was in prayer.

Moments later, the roar of an engine caught their attention, and their heads swiveled in unison to look out the large front bay window as an ambulance pulled up. It was all white with a red roof, the front round wheel wells merged with running boards that had seen some wear and tear. A single light just above the windshield flashed red. Two men wearing white jackets and red caps hopped out and ran around to the back of the wagon, where they unloaded an empty stretcher. They rushed inside the medical center, steering the stretcher between them. They disappeared down the hall, in the direction of where Herschel had been deposited. Instantly, Mickey and Daniel were on their feet.

"What do you think is happening?" Mickey asked.

"I don't know, but I don't think it's good." Daniel immediately started making a contingency plan in his head. If Herschel Ross was seriously injured or—heaven forbid—dead, then he would most likely be out of a job. He'd have to move back to Fort Collins and find work there. Suddenly, an image of Colleen flooded his mind at the very thought of leaving Havenwood Falls. Like his heart was held in a vise that was being tightened, pain pierced his chest. He doubled over gasping, and when Mickey whipped his head around, Daniel covered it up with a cough.

"You okay, Hoss?" Mickey asked, a thick dark eyebrow arched in question.

"Yeah, I think I strained a muscle carrying our boss." Forcing himself to stand up straight, he winced and rubbed the area over his chest that still burned.

A flurry of activity exploded in the hallway as Herschel Ross was wheeled out, strapped to the gurney. Nurse Heller rushed after them and passed off a dark brown file to one of the medics like she was passing a baton in a relay race. Within seconds, Herschel was loaded into the back of the ambulance. With sirens blaring and tires squealing, the rig raced off into the night.

As the siren faded, Daniel began to accept that he would have to move again. The idea didn't appeal to him. Despite finding his mate and discovering she was human, Daniel was beginning to like Havenwood Falls.

"Where's he going?" Mickey asked.

"Grand Junction. His injuries are too severe to treat here. His jaw will most likely need to be wired shut, and I suspect he has bleeding on his brain. One of his pupils was dilated and the other was fine, which is a good indicator without taking X-rays," Nurse Heller said. "I really shouldn't be telling you since you're not kin, but Herschel doesn't have anyone, and you found him."

They made to leave, but Nurse Heller called out. "Hold tight, boys, the sheriff's going to want to talk to you."

Daniel paused and swallowed deep. He hadn't thought about a crime having been committed, and here he was, new in town without anyone to vouch for him except for Mickey, but how well did he know Mickey? Would the sheriff be like other small-town cops and find someone easy to pin the blame on?

Minutes later, a sleek black truck with whitewall tires came to a stop in front of the medical center. A large man stepped out and adjusted his gun belt. He wore jeans and a denim shirt with the sleeves rolled up to his elbows, the gold star badge reflecting the overhead lighting the only indication this man was law enforcement. As the officer walked toward the waiting area, he tipped his tan cowboy hat at Nurse Heller, who blushed before pretending to be busy shuffling papers at the registration desk.

"Mickey," he said and pulled out a small notepad from his back pocket. "And you must be Daniel McCabe." Piercing blue eyes landed on Daniel, and a blast of wolf washed over him as the sheriff projected his scent, sending a message that in addition to sheriff, he was also a wolf shifter.

"Yes, sir," Daniel answered, standing straighter and squaring his shoulders, not only hiding his surprise, but sending his own message that he wouldn't be pushed around. They eyeballed each other, and Mickey shifted nervously next to Daniel the longer the stare down lasted. The sheriff finally smirked and extended his hand.

"Sheriff Ric Kasun. You mind telling me what happened?"

Daniel shook his hand, making sure his grip was tight, then he and Mickey launched into telling Sheriff Kasun where they discovered Herschel.

An hour later, satisfied with their answers, Sheriff Kasun dismissed them.

Insects danced in the beam from his truck's headlights as Daniel drove back to the cabin with eyelids so heavy, they threatened to close. Normally he had more energy at night, a side effect of being part feline, but his emotions had been all over the map. Once he was away from the town center, darkness descended, and he struggled to focus. When he turned off on the dirt road that led to the cabins, he slowed down. Trees loomed on either side of the road, their bark looking like leathery skin when illuminated by the headlights.

Stumbling into the cabin, he tossed his keys on the small rustic dining table and continued straight into the bedroom. Within minutes, he was asleep.

Chirping birds and the early tendrils of morning sunshine woke Daniel from a restless slumber. He sat up in bed, the top sheet pooling around his waist. Looking around, he noticed his clothes on the floor where he had stripped them off before climbing into bed. His sheets were clean, with no evidence of dirt and leaves, which meant he hadn't shifted and gone roaming the forest to stand in the shadows, watching Colleen's house. Relieved it was just a dream, he let out a sigh and fell back against the pillows.

As he lay there, he thought about Herschel and how the man's health left his job hanging in the balance. Daniel looked around the room. His suitcase was open on the floor next to the dresser. He hadn't bothered to unpack yet, so it would be easy to pick up and leave. He was used to it.

Sitting up, he swung his legs over the side of the bed. His feet landed on the hardwood floor. Scratching his head, he walked to the window that looked out upon the forest that surrounded the cabin. A light breeze caused tree tops to sway, and birds swooped and flew in their own random dance. A deer stepped out from the tree line and froze, its head raised and eyes alert as it surveyed the area before crossing a small meadow and disappearing into the trees on the other side. Daniel tracked the deer's movement, the urge to hunt surfacing briefly before his humanity shut it down. How easy it would be to slip out the back door and shift without being seen, but as the sun rose higher in the sky, the urge to hunt faded. He knew he'd have to soon, though. It had been almost a week since his last kill. The longer he went without hunting, the harder it became to curb his urges, and his mountain lion became difficult to contain.

That was one of the things that appealed to him when Elsmed Fairchild explained Havenwood Falls and how the supernaturals coexisted with humans. He still had to be careful about displaying anything unusual in public, but protections were in place to avoid anything catastrophic. Knowing he would be leaving those safeguards behind, as well as his mate, hurt more than he imagined.

Despite the internal objections from his mountain lion, Daniel turned away from the window and crossed the bedroom. He hoisted his suitcase onto the bed and tossed in the few things he had unpacked.

CHAPTER 7

*D*isappointment hung around Colleen's neck like a weight, causing her shoulders to droop. She scrunched the paper bag from her lunch into a ball. With her book tucked under her arm, she walked along the brick walkway that wove through Town Square Park. As she left the square, she tossed the paper bag into a trash bin before waiting at the intersection to cross the street. Daniel hadn't shown up for lunch at the bench as she had hoped.

Apparently, the attraction was one-sided. She doubted he dreamed about her at night the way she did about him. Dreams that left her wanting. Dreams that made her entire body hum and her skin flush from heat that burned deep within. Every morning that week, she woke up feeling like she needed to go directly to church and confess her sins. Did impure thoughts count when they were your subconscious and the thoughts occurred in dreams? She was a good girl, still a virgin and planned on staying that way until her wedding night. The night before, she dreamt she was pregnant and Daniel stood behind her, cupping her swollen breasts. She woke up completely off kilter and longing to see the man who was still a stranger to her in reality, but so familiar to her in her dreams. By the time her lunch break rolled around, Colleen was practically crawling out of her skin with anticipation of seeing Daniel and getting to know him more. She kept checking her watch and scanning the square looking for him, her book abandoned on the bench next to her. But he never showed.

Sighing, she pushed open the door to her family's market. The bell chimed, announcing her entrance, and her dad looked up from the register.

"Hi, pumpkin, what's wrong?" He peered at her over his bifocals. Slapping a smile in place, she walked over to him.

"I'm fine, Daddy. Just a little tired is all. It sure is warm out there today." Nothing distracted her father more than talking about the weather. He could spend hours gabbing with customers over the ice storm of '39 or the drought of the summer of '46.

"They say it could be a record breaker. I better bring in an extra fan from out back." Just like that, he was gone, and Colleen let her smile fall as she slipped her store apron over her head and tied the strings around her slim waist.

At around two in the afternoon on Fridays is when business started to pick up. People stopped in for last minute dinner items or to grab things for the weekend. When school was in session, it became even busier at three, when students came in after school to raid the penny candy display and buy bottles of pop. Colleen was ringing people up when she overheard how Herschel Ross had been assaulted, nearly beaten to death and dumped in a dirt lot like a piece of garbage. When she heard Daniel's name mentioned, her ears perked up.

"That new foreman, Daniel McCabe, and Mickey Ahusaka found him. They carried him to the medical center, bless them," Hilary Monroe shared with Melba Ferguson, who stood in line behind her.

"What do we know about this Daniel McCabe?"

"He's a mystery. Patty Parker refuses to say. She acts all high and mighty, claiming employee confidentiality. I think we should pay him a visit." Melba Ferguson and Hilary Monroe were on the town's unofficial welcoming committee and two of the town's biggest busybodies.

"I think we should. Will he be around, though?"

"Patty did say he is going to step in and help run things until Herschel has recovered," Hilary added.

"Is he still in a coma?" Melba asked.

"A coma? I hadn't heard that!"

"Well, Cindy Adams heard it from Calista Harmon at the library bake sale this morning . . ."

Colleen rolled her eyes at the gossip mill. Calista owned Callie's Trinkets, a designer consignment store around the corner from the market. Her shop was frequented by just about every housewife in Havenwood Falls. Colleen knew from watching her mother's friends, whenever it was her mom's turn to host bridge club, that idle housewives loved to talk. By tomorrow, Herschel will have achieved martyr status even though he was probably one of the biggest jerks in town. Whenever he walked through the door of the market, she had to brace herself, because he inevitably would complain about something just to get a discount. He liked to wink at her and make suggestive comments, too. One piece of information she overheard, that Daniel was staying on as foreman, she hoped was true and not a rumor.

After closing, Colleen straightened items on the shelves and made notes on what needed to be restocked or reordered. She wiped down the cooler doors of the hundreds of fingerprints and smudges on the glass, counted down the drawer, and swept the floors. Her dad was in the back office when she went to retrieve her change of clothes. She was meeting her friend Sally Andrews at Burger Bar to talk about Peggy's wedding. Sally was a bridesmaid and had offered to help plan the bridal shower.

"All set?" her dad asked, looking up from the ledger when Colleen set the bag of cash and checks in front of him.

"Yes. I'm going to meet Sal at Burger Bar."

"That's nice. Be safe."

"I will, Daddy." She leaned over the desk and kissed the top of his head, which was already bent over the ledger again.

Grabbing her bag, she slipped into the restroom and changed out of her capris, slipping on a black pencil skirt that stopped just below her knees. She pulled on a hot-pink short-sleeved knit top. Looking in the mirror, she fluffed her hair and put on a little bit of makeup, just a touch of mascara and pink lipstick. She kept her saddle shoes on because her feet ached after standing all day.

Less than ten minutes later, she was entering Burger Bar, bypassing the area where people parked their cars and placed their orders. There was a separate dining area like a regular restaurant. The juke box was blaring "Be-Bop-A-Lula" by Gene Vincent, which put a little sway in her step as she crossed the black and white checkerboard floor to the booth where Sally was sitting. Her friend wore a yellow blouse that stood out like a beacon, making her easy to spot. Sally's thick brown hair was pulled back in a ponytail and she wore tortoiseshell horn-rimmed glasses that framed gorgeous hazel eyes. Sally was sipping on a Coke when Colleen slid into the booth.

"I'm starved!" Colleen proclaimed and snagged a menu from the end of the table, even though she already knew what she was going to order. She always ordered the same thing: a regular cheeseburger with pickles on the side, French fries, and a Coke.

Sally shook her head and laughed.

"What?" Colleen asked, scanning through the limited options.

"You always order the same thing. Why bother looking at the menu?"

Colleen shrugged and set the menu down on the Formica table. "Maybe something will jump out at me. You make me sound predictable."

Sally snorted. "That's because you are! That's okay. I still think you're swell."

Colleen frowned at her friend's opinion. She was too young to be considered predictable. Granted, there weren't a lot of options to do anything wild in Havenwood Falls, except run with the Greasers who liked to drag race on Blackstone Road late at night. There weren't any homes along the stretch that ran between County Road and Havenwood Heights, the upscale neighborhood where most of the old money families lived. She could spend time at the Haven Saloon, but she didn't want to just drink in a bar. That wasn't fun for her, and darts . . . well, darts could be dangerous. Throwing sharp objects through the air while inebriated didn't seem like a good idea.

A waitress came by to take her usual order and rushed off. Friday nights were always busy. Colleen glanced around to see who all was there. Herne Fairchild was sitting at the booth across from hers. He lived down the street from her and his looks always made her pause. With his blond hair, blue eyes, and bright white smile, he reminded her of a model from a Sears & Roebuck catalog, right down to his perfectly creased chinos.

The Bishop brothers, Ronan and Roman, were in another booth. They were a few years older than Colleen and both incredibly handsome, with dark hair and blue, stormy eyes. The Bishop family helped to found Havenwood Falls. With their looks and old money, either one of the brothers would have been a good catch, except there was something about them. They made her think of a bright red apple that looked perfect on the outside, but hid bruises and rotten spots just underneath the skin.

A man sat in the corner of the restaurant, and Colleen's lips parted in surprise. She had never seen Viktor Azimov at Burger Bar before. He was always an interesting character—very dark and brooding with thick black hair and eyes a bottomless midnight blue that stood out against skin as white as milk. In the winter, he wore a long black wool coat with a tall top hat, reminiscent of Abraham Lincoln, and he cut a striking figure whenever he walked through town. When Viktor passed by one of the gas-lit streetlamps, he seemed like a ghost from a different era. Now he wore a black leather jacket over a black shirt and denim jeans. His table was empty except for an untouched strawberry milkshake. Ice cream dripped down the side of the glass, and it looked like wax on a candle. He was in observation mode, too, and as if he felt Colleen watching, his dark eyes met hers. Blood rushed to her cheeks when she blushed, and she quickly looked away, embarrassed that she was caught staring.

The waitress returned with her dinner, and Colleen placed her napkin across her lap before diving in with both hands. Sally filled her in on how she spoke to Irina Petran at the Whisper Falls Inn and secured the dining area for Peggy's bridal shower. They were going with a traditional tea party theme and agreed the majestic Victorian inn would be the perfect venue. Once they mapped out a list of what needed to be done and who should be invited, Sally steered the conversation back to Colleen's predictability. Sally's hazel eyes glittered mischievously behind her glasses, and she flashed a sly grin.

"Sally, no. Whatever it is you're thinking, no. The last time you had that look, I snorted salt up my nose on a dare."

Sally pouted and crossed her arms on the table. "You're no fun."

Just then, someone came to a stop next their table, and Colleen's nose filled with the most delicious scent. It was like dark chocolate and raspberry. The two women peered up at the man standing beside them. Up close, Viktor Azimov literally took Colleen's breath away. His skin was flawless perfection. His lips were full, his cheekbones sharp, and his eyes hypnotizing. Once she met his gaze, she couldn't look away.

"Dance with me?" he asked and held out a hand to her. "In the Still of the Night" had just started playing on the jukebox. An internal voice urged her to look away and to decline his offer. She opened her mouth, starting to form the word no, when Sally answered for her.

"She'd love to. I was just telling her she needs to live a little."

Viktor smiled, exposing a glimpse of really bright teeth. They practically reflected the light.

"No. I really can't." Colleen managed to break eye contact and nervously fidgeted with the napkin on her lap.

"One dance can't hurt, Colleen. Go. I dare you." Sally winked at her, and Colleen sighed dramatically.

"Fine." She tossed the napkin on the table and slid out of the booth. "One dance." She placed her hand in Viktor's and almost yanked it back. His skin was ice cold. Before she could pull away, his fingers wrapped around hers, and he was tugging her over to a small area where tables had been moved to the side to make room for dancing.

Viktor moved in close and placed his hands on Colleen's hips. She put her hands on his shoulders. He was much taller than her, and she had to shuffle a bit closer to ease the stretch in her arms. His dark hair was just long enough to brush along the tops of her hands. Chocolate, raspberry, and the heavy scent of leather from his jacket washed over her, and Colleen closed her eyes. She didn't realize she was nuzzling his neck until the music switched to "Tutti Frutti." The upbeat tempo and Little Richard's raspy howl broke through her haze. Her heart was beating so fast, and she felt her cheeks heat with embarrassment. Viktor looked at her like he wanted to devour her, the way she had looked at her cheeseburger.

"Come with me," Viktor said. His voice was clear as day over the music, yet she could have sworn his full lips hadn't moved. Dazed, she nodded and turned to say goodbye to Sally, who was staring at them like the Cheshire cat.

"Go live a little, Colleen. Be unpredictable."

Viktor led her through the crowded restaurant and outside. The cool night air was a relief against her hot cheeks, and she took a few deep breaths that helped to clear her head. She came to a stop, and Viktor's hand almost slipped from hers, but he clamped down at the last second and turned to look at her. Once again, their eyes met, and any doubts about leaving with Viktor disappeared. Tucked in the back corner of the parking lot, a black Corvette shone in the moonlight. Had it been a cloudy night, the convertible would have been camouflaged in the shadows of two cottonwood trees.

Viktor held the door open for her, and Colleen sunk down onto red leather. The convertible top was down, and Colleen held her hair back to keep it from blowing in her face. Taking a left on Farnsworth Road, just before the turnoff to Blackstone Road, Viktor sped along until he reached the covered bridge. The road led to an abandoned mine and was hardly ever used. Inside the bridge, the sound of rushing water from Mathews River was amplified. Leaving the radio and headlights on, Viktor put the car in park and in one swift movement, wrapped his arm around Colleen's shoulders and leaned in close.

"You smell amazing," he said and buried his nose in her hair. "Did you know hamburgers are a good source of iron?"

What a strange thing to say, she thought, but was immediately distracted when Viktor slid a hand beneath her top and skimmed his fingers along her back, his icy touch making her shiver.

"Let me kiss you," he breathed in her ear. "I need to taste you."

The longing in his voice made her breath hitch. Her thoughts weren't her own from that point on.

"Yes, please. Kiss me," she practically begged, slamming an imaginary door on the inner voice that was screaming in her head, telling her to run, effectively reducing it to muffled sounds of protest.

Viktor's mouth descended upon hers. His tongue teased the seam of her lips, and she opened for him. His tongue was cool at first, but after a few seconds of the deeper kiss, everything warmed up. He sucked her bottom lip between his teeth, and she gasped at the pinching sensation, but the pain quickly changed to pleasure that traveled down deep. He sucked and sucked. With each pull on her lip, something built inside of her that felt incredibly wrong, but also so good.

A sharp cry of a hawk pierced the night, startling Colleen. The way the call echoed, it sounded close, like the hawk was under the covered bridge with them. It startled her enough that she pulled away. Viktor released her lip with a pop, and she scooted away from him, appalled at her brazen behavior. Raising her fingers to her lips, she discovered they were hot and swollen to the touch. Viktor's eyes looked almost completely black. Blaming it on a trick of the shadows, she quickly looked away.

"I'd like to go home now," she said, her voice huskier than usual. Viktor brushed her hair away from her cheek, his hand much warmer than before, and she felt him observing her as if waiting for her to change her mind. She refused to look at him, afraid of losing control again. Sally wanted Colleen to live a little; well, this definitely had to count. She licked her lips, tasting chocolate and something rich, almost metallic.

Honoring her request, Viktor drove her home. They didn't say anything to each other, and as soon as he pulled up in front of her house, she climbed out of the car and ran up the brick walkway to the front porch. She heard the low purr of the Corvette as he left, and she ducked inside her house, staying in the foyer until her breathing and her pulse were under control. It was after eleven, and her family was already asleep. She quietly climbed the stairs, avoiding the spot that always squeaked, and once Colleen was in her bedroom with the door closed, she collapsed on the bed. Touching her lips again, she discovered they were still swollen and a little sore. Shame washed over her when she realized she had never even properly introduced herself to Viktor. He didn't know her name. They didn't know anything about each other, and she let him paw at her like she was easy pickings. A vision of Daniel popped into her head, and the sense of shame deepened, as if she had actually been unfaithful to yet another man who was a stranger.

"I'm losing my mind," she whispered and curled up in a ball in the middle of her bed, where she fell into a fitful sleep.

CHAPTER 8

*J*ust as Daniel had climbed into bed, ready to get some sleep for his long drive back to Fort Collins the next morning, there was a sharp knock on the front door. He looked at his clock. It was almost eleven, and since he didn't know too many people in town, he had no idea who was paying him a visit. Lifting his nose in the air, he breathed in deep, separating the layers of scents around him and picking up on a familiar one: Mickey.

He opened the door to find Mickey wearing shorts and nothing else. His hair was free of the leather band he usually tied it back with when they were working. It hung loose in thick dark waves around his broad shoulders. Sensing agitation rolling off his friend, Daniel quickly invited him in.

"What's going on?"

"The other night you said your mate was Colleen Campbell, right?"

"Yes, why?"

Mickey paced the tiny living room, his heavy footsteps causing the hardwood floor to vibrate.

"She was making out with Viktor Asimov. He was feeding off of her."

Daniel's blood ran cold, and he placed his hands on Mickey's shoulders, forcing him to stop pacing.

"Who is Viktor, and what the hell do you mean he was feeding?"

"Viktor is the head of the Gothic vampire nest here in Havenwood Falls. I think he compelled her to go with him."

"Tell me everything," Daniel demanded. His hands curled into fists. Claws burst through the tips of his fingers, piercing his palms, the pain helping him to keep from shifting as Mickey told him he had been flying overhead. That's what he did—he was a watcher and kept watch from above. He saw Colleen leave Burger Bar with the vampire. He followed them to the covered bridge. His cry had interrupted them when things were getting hot and heavy.

"When they drove away, I flew right here. If she's your fated mate, you need to know. Viktor tends to lure humans in and make them his blood slaves."

"The Court allows this?"

Mickey shrugged. "He doesn't kill them, and he needs blood to survive. He might be looking to recruit Colleen."

Daniel growled, which his inner cat echoed. Stripping out of his underwear, he let his mountain lion free and shifted there in the living room. He didn't even feel the pain this time, he was so focused on getting to Colleen and making sure she was safe. He bounded out the front door and heard a hawk cry overhead. Looking up, he barely made out Mickey's dark wings against the night sky.

Daniel ran along the river until he reached the trees that surrounded Colleen's backyard. He paused, ears flicking back and forth as he listened for any witnesses or threats. All was quiet except for the rustle of feathers as Mickey settled on a branch above his head. Crouched down low and alert, he stole forward and approached the back of the house. A faint trace of vampire scent was in the air, and he followed it around the side of the house to the curb. The vampire hadn't breached the walls. This was good.

Mine ran on repeat in his head at the idea of a vampire touching his mate, taking her blood. His cat wanted to send a message, and before Daniel could assert his will over his animal, he was spraying the front bushes and proceeded to spray the perimeter of the house, marking his territory with musky urine. Daniel ran back into the woods and traced his steps back to the cabin, with Mickey following him. As soon as he was inside his cabin, he shifted back to his human form. Mickey flew in behind and shifted mid-air, coming to a running stop like a skydiver. He doubled over laughing, slapping at his bare thigh.

"You peed on her bushes! That's a riot!"

"Just staking my claim."

"So, you've decided then, you're going to pursue her?" Mickey asked as he pulled on his shorts that had been left on the floor.

"Yeah, I am." At that proclamation, his inner cat let out a contented purr and settled down. His reaction to another supernatural sniffing around his mate made it clear, and he couldn't deny it any longer. As far as Colleen being a human, he'd have to find a way to make it work.

Daniel bent over and picked up his underwear and slipped them on, covering up his nakedness. Nudity didn't bother shifters, though, so he wasn't uncomfortable around Mickey. He understood.

"All right, I need to get some shut-eye. It's at least a seven-hour drive tomorrow."

"So, are you going to stay on as foreman, run things until Mr. Ross is back?"

Daniel nodded. "I'm going to get my mom. She needs to see Havenwood Falls. I think she'll be happy here. We'll be back sometime Sunday."

"See you then."

As Mickey turned to leave, Daniel called to him. "Thanks for looking out for Colleen. Do you mind keeping an eye on her while I'm gone?"

Mickey grinned. "That's what friends are for." With a final wave, he slipped out into the night.

Shutting the door behind his friend, Daniel smiled. Assimilating to life in Havenwood Falls was surprisingly easy. Mickey was proving to be a loyal friend, already looking out for his interests. It had been a long time since Daniel allowed himself the luxury of friendship.

CHAPTER 9

Something hit the side of the house beneath Colleen's bedroom window, waking her up. Sunlight streamed in through her windows, the pink gingham curtains blowing in a light breeze. She climbed out of bed and crossed her room to see what hit the house. Looking down on the backyard below, she saw her mom, hose in hand, spraying down her roses. The sound that had woken Colleen was the water hitting the house.

Colleen quickly showered and dressed for work before going downstairs. Her mom had left a place setting at the small dinette table, which was located in the far corner of the kitchen, close to the back door. She poured some Chex in a bowl and grabbed a bottle of milk from the refrigerator. Taking her breakfast with her outside, she discovered her sister was sitting on the small deck, reading.

"Mom, didn't you water the roses yesterday?" Colleen asked, taking a seat next to her sister.

Her mom stopped the spray of water and glanced up, tilting her wide brimmed gardening hat away from her eyes so she could see.

"I did, but some animal sprayed them last night—sprayed around the entire house—and it smells awful."

Colleen sniffed the air and shrugged. "It doesn't smell bad, almost like cinnamon or cloves."

Kelly snorted. "Cinnamon? Have you gone mad? It smells like a bunch of feral cats had a party last night."

"Are you sure it wasn't David, Mom? You know he liked to pee in the backyard when he was little. What if the neighbors saw him?" Kelly hid her laughing face behind her book.

"Girls," their mom responded with a shake of her head, "I'm pretty sure I would have heard about your brother peeing in the bushes by now. Especially since I already heard about you leaving Burger Bar with Viktor Asimov last night."

Her mom stood with her hands on her hips. She was still holding the hose in one hand, looped out from her side like a lasso.

"Really?" Kelly's eyes were huge as she leaned toward her sister.

Colleen blushed and groaned. "Honestly, this town. Rumors spread faster than wildfire. It's just like Peyton Place. It's a wonder anyone can keep a secret around here!"

"Are you and Viktor in looooove?" Kelly asked, making kissy sounds at her.

"No. It was one kiss, and I don't plan on seeing him again."

"Good," her mom said. "I won't have any of my daughters running around with strange men. Your father and I didn't raise you to be that way."

"Ugh, honestly, mother, you think anyone who dresses differently and who doesn't attend at least one church social is strange." Colleen stood up, her empty bowl in hand. "I'm going to be late for work." She stomped across the deck, kissy sounds following her into the house.

Pedaling her bicycle to work helped to calm her down, and by the time she was propping her bike up against the lamppost in front of the store, she had a genuine smile on her face.

How quickly that smile faded when she overheard several of the ladies who were in her mother's bridge club gossiping about Daniel. Two of the women, Melba Ferguson and Hilary Monroe, were full of information. Apparently, Melba had gone over to the cabin where Daniel was staying with one of her famous apple pies to welcome him to Havenwood Falls, but was too late. She saw him loading a suitcase into his truck right before he drove out of town.

"Such a shame," Melba said. "I'm beginning to wonder if Miller's Plaza will ever be built."

"Oh, don't you worry, Melba," Patty Parker chimed in. She reached across Hilary and plucked a can of Kitchen Klenzer off the shelf. She briefly examined the label before placing the can in her basket. "I have it on good authority that Daniel is staying on as foreman. He just went to go pick up his mother to bring her here for a visit."

"So he does have family?" Hilary asked.

"Yes, it's just him and his mother. His father died a few years ago. He's been taking care of her ever since—he simply dotes on her."

"Oh, the poor dear."

"So tragic," Hilary said with a sigh.

"She's lucky to have such a devoted son," Mrs. Wilson said with a sniff. Her son, Wally, had left Havenwood Falls right after he graduated high school and never came back.

"He isn't married. I wonder who we can introduce him to? He'd make a fine match for someone."

The ladies moved to the next aisle, and Colleen strained to hear who they were hypothesizing about. The very idea of them playing matchmaker with Daniel made her want to yell at them to mind their own business, that Daniel was hers. Surprised at the possessiveness of her thoughts, Colleen ground her teeth together to avoid an embarrassing outburst and regarded the gossipers through narrow eyes. Patty stepped forward to the register, setting her basket down on the counter.

"Relax, dear." She placed her hand on top of Colleen's, which was curled into a tight fist. "You have nothing to worry about," she said cryptically and winked.

Before Colleen could ask her what she meant, Patty was walking away, the brown paper grocery bag tucked against her hip like she was carrying a child.

That afternoon was busy since it was the second Saturday of the month, which was when Movies in the Park took place. Havenwood Falls was too small to justify a drive-in movie theater, so the city council and local businesses created the next best thing. Practically the whole town gathered to watch a recent family-friendly flick, and then adults and teenagers stayed for the second movie. That weekend they were showing *Tarzan and the Lost Safari* first, followed by *I Was a Teenage Werewolf*. The latter had created quite the buzz with all of the female high school students because the actor, Michael Landon, was positively dreamy. Colleen laughed out loud when she realized that what her brother David and his friend saw by the river the other day wasn't a wolf with glowing eyes, but just a figment of their imagination. They had been obsessed with this movie. Hollywood and books featured creatures of the night and shape-shifting beasts, but she knew they didn't exist in real life.

The market usually closed at seven, but by six thirty it was dead, so her dad decided to close early. Colleen stayed at the front of the store cleaning and straightening for over an hour while her dad went to the back office to do some paperwork. When she was done, she peeked her head in his office and waited until he finished counting out a stack of money before telling him goodbye.

"I'll be over in a bit, pumpkin. Save me some popcorn."

Colleen promised she would and reminded him to put her bicycle in the back of the station wagon. After hanging up her apron and grabbing her purse, she went back through the market and out the front door, making sure to lock it. She stepped onto the sidewalk and froze in place when she saw a sleek black Corvette parked alongside the curb. The convertible top was down, and Viktor sat behind the steering wheel. He had an arm stretched out along the front seat and his other arm propped against the top of the door. This position put him at the perfect angle to watch the market entrance.

"Viktor, what are you doing here?"

"I came to see you." He got out of his car and moved toward her. The way he walked, with his intense dark eyes focused on her, he came across as predatory, and she instinctively took a step back. Just then, she heard someone running, and she turned to see Mickey Ahusaka running down the sidewalk, his hair streaming behind him like a thick, black ribbon. He came to a sudden stop, in between her and Viktor.

"Shoot, you're closed?" he asked, looking over her shoulder at the darkened storefront window.

"Yes, we are. Sorry."

Mickey frowned and let out a sigh. "My mom called because my little brother is sick. Since I live around the corner, she asked me to pick up some Pepto-Bismol."

Colleen glanced at her watch. The movie would be starting at eight thirty, once the sun set. She still had time.

"Come on," she said and pulled the store keys out of her purse. "We can't let Nahele suffer all night." Unlocking the door, she flicked on the lights and called to her dad, knowing he would have heard the bell above the door. She crossed to the hygiene and home remedy aisle to grab a bottle of Pepto. "Is one bottle enough?" she asked Mickey.

When he didn't answer, she looked up to discover he wasn't in the store. Walking over to the window, she peered out and saw him talking to Viktor. It didn't look like a friendly conversation either, by the way they squared off. Seconds later, Viktor spun around and climbed into his car. Mickey watched him leave before coming into the store.

"Sorry," he said.

"What was that all about?"

"Nothing." Mickey shrugged nonchalantly, and Colleen didn't believe him for a second. She knew male posturing when she saw it, and if she wasn't mistaken, Mickey scared Viktor off, but why? "Thanks for opening the store back up. You're a real peach." He flashed a brilliant smile, which stood out against his darker skin.

They walked out together. Mickey stood with his shoulders hunched and hands in the pockets of his Levi's as he waited for her to lock the door. She pulled on the handle, double checking that it was secure.

"Well, good night, Mickey. I hope that fixes your brother right up." Colleen made to leave.

"Going to the movies?" Mickey asked, catching up to her at the crosswalk. Colleen nodded and started across the street, since there weren't any cars in sight. "I'll walk with you."

"Don't you have to get that to your brother?" She glanced at his hand holding the bottle of pink medicine.

"I'll see you safely to the park first."

"If you insist." Colleen shook her head, unable to imagine what dangers Mickey thought she'd encounter on the short walk.

Picking her way in between people sitting on the grass, using only the flickering light from the giant movie screen to see, Colleen made her way to the large oak tree, where her family had planned to sit. Mickey followed her like a shadow. Pausing occasionally, Colleen was distracted by the movie. She had arrived just as a plane had crashed and Tarzan, a big strapping beast of a man wearing only a loincloth, heroically rescued the passengers. She found her family sitting on a large plaid picnic blanket. Her mom had brought a Tupperware container of popcorn and a cooler full of bottles of Coca-Cola. Once Colleen was situated next to her sister, Mickey whispered good night.

"What was that all about?" Kelly asked. "Are you kissing him, too?"

"No!" she hissed, thankful it was dark so nobody saw her cheeks flare red.

Her dad joined them not too long after, and they finished watching the movie. Once it was over, her parents left. They didn't have any interest in watching a horror movie about a bunch of teenagers.

"We already know what living with teenagers is like," her dad joked before leaving. As soon as they left, Kelly slipped away to hang with her friends and to swoon over Michael Landon. David's friend Billy appeared out of nowhere and immediately descended upon the popcorn. Colleen stood up to stretch, and that's when she noticed Mickey's brother sitting not even twenty feet away, looking as healthy as a horse. This caused her brow to wrinkle in confusion. Between Patty, Viktor, and Mickey, just what the hell was going on?

CHAPTER 10

$\mathcal{H}$aving only been back in Fort Collins for one night, Daniel already missed the peacefulness of Havenwood Falls. He hadn't realized how loud and confining city living could be. Being around more people, more traffic, more noise, more everything made his skin crawl. How quickly he had adjusted to his temporary cabin in the woods.

Shuffling into the kitchen, following the smell of coffee percolating on the stove, he smiled when he saw his mom stirring a pan full of eggs.

"I missed your cooking," he said, kissing her on the cheek before reaching over her head to grab a mug out of the cabinet.

"Soon you'll find yourself a wife, and you'll only want her cooking," she teased. At the mention of a wife, Daniel's shoulders tightened. He felt them draw up like he was a puppet on a string. Of course, his mom noticed. She didn't miss anything. "Daniel?"

Sighing, he sat down at the table and wrapped his large hands around the mug. He hadn't told her about Colleen, because he was still coming to terms with finding his mate. His mom carried the pan of eggs over and dropped several scoopfuls on his plate. A platter of bacon and toast was already on the table. He grabbed several slices as his mom sat down across from him.

"Is there something you're not telling me?" she pried.

Daniel finished chewing and swallowing before answering. "I found my mate, Mom, in Havenwood Falls."

"Oh, that's wonderful, Danny!" She set her fork down and reached across the table, giving his hand a squeeze. "What are the odds—a new job and finding your mate, all in the same week." She must have seen the conflict written on his face, because when she looked at him, her expression morphed into one of concern. "What's wrong? This should be a joyous occasion."

"I know, it's just, well, it's complicated."

"How so?"

"She's human."

His mom paused and slowly brought the napkin up from her lap and wiped the corner of her mouth. "Well, I can see that would be a complication if she doesn't know shifters exist, but it won't be the first interspecies relationship. We're compatible with humans."

"That's just it, Mom. We're not compatible. Humans are dangerous. What if I tell her and she flips out? Next thing you know, I'm either being put down or I'm held prisoner in a government lab somewhere, being experimented on."

"Oh, Danny, no! God damn him!"

Daniel sat back in shock when his mom threw her napkin on the table and stood up.

"Who?"

"Your father."

"What? Why?" Now it was Daniel's turn to jump up out of his chair.

She started to clear the table, angrily scraping food into the trash can. Filling up the sink with hot sudsy water, she tossed the dishes in, sending a burst of bubbles into the air. Daniel had seen this reaction many times before. Whenever his mom was angry or upset, she cleaned. She scrubbed every surface until she calmed down. It took a few minutes for that moment to come. Finally, with her head lowered and shoulders hunched, she dropped the dishcloth in the soapy water.

"I love your father, but . . . ," she started, turning around to face him. Tears shimmered in her blue eyes, but they didn't spill. "His mistrust, his fear of humans—he poisoned you with it. His experience in Sunset Creek shaped his entire life. I could never understand, because my childhood was normal, safe. I've never felt hunted or threatened. Your father and I argued something fierce about how he was letting his prejudices rub off on you." She sighed and smoothed the skirt on her pale blue dress before crossing the room to sit back down in her chair. "Not all humans are bad. You know that. You've worked alongside them, gone to school with them."

"I know that," Daniel said, sitting down across from her. "But I kept my distance and for good reason. Remember, in Kentucky, that colored man who was beaten for making a pass at a white woman? Remember the segregation? All because of different skin color." Daniel cringed whenever he saw a sign posted at a business announcing it was for whites only. It didn't take much to imagine a sign that read "humans only." He didn't see that ever happening in Havenwood Falls, though. There the supernatural went about their lives unbeknownst to the humans.

"Don't you realize how hypocritical you sound?" she asked. "You're just as prejudiced, and I'm sorry I didn't raise you better. Despite our arguments, it wasn't my place to go against your father. There was no convincing him, and he became set in his ways, but there has to be hope for you, Danny. This girl is your mate for a reason. Human or shifter, you have to learn to accept her."

"I'm trying, Mom. I'm going to ask Colleen out on a date and see how things go. With her being human, is it even possible she can feel the same mating call? Besides, someone else has been sniffing around her, and I can't let that stand." If he was in his mountain lion form, his hackles would have been raised. Just the thought of another man, let alone another species, making moves on his mate made him see red.

"Daniel Matthew McCabe, you need to go claim your mate!" His mom chastised him and stood up. "Let's go. We need to get you back to Havenwood Falls. Good thing I packed already. I can't wait to see this town."

Daniel went to his room and grabbed more clothes from his closet.

The Court had granted him a special pass to leave Havenwood Falls without immediately losing his memories of the town. It had taken a few minutes for his temporary tattoo to be enhanced, and the instructions were firm: as long as he was back before midnight on Monday, he would be fine. Looking around his room, he knew it wouldn't take much to move. They had moved so much that their possessions were few, and they often never unpacked completely. His parents' china set, a wedding present from his mom's parents, was stowed away in a box in the hallway closet. His bedroom walls were bare, with the exception of the green-and-brown-striped wallpaper. The few pictures he had were on the top of his four-drawer dresser. There was a large framed picture of his mom and dad when they were first mated. Another picture was of Daniel when he was three years old. He sat in a straight-backed rocking chair with his baby sister, Katherine, on his lap, holding on to her so tight you could see the strain in his smile. According to his parents, Katherine passed away just six months later from pneumonia. He had vague memories of her, mainly just her scent, which was imprinted on him. After the first warm spring rain caused blossoms to open and sweetened the air, he always thought of her.

Snapping out of the memories, he closed his suitcase. No, it wouldn't take much to move, and he had a feeling he'd be moving to Havenwood Falls permanently. His mountain lion rumbled in agreement.

WHEN DANIEL PULLED up to the cabin later that afternoon, Mickey was waiting for him. He sat on the front steps wearing Levi's that were folded at the bottom, forming wide cuffs. He was barefoot, and his shirt was partially unbuttoned. Daniel recognized the disheveled look as someone who had recently shifted and put their clothes on in a hurry.

He climbed out of the truck and briefly stretched before walking around to the passenger side to open the door for his mom. She'd brain him if he forgot his manners.

Mickey sauntered over to meet them.

"Mickey, this is my mom, Margaret McCabe. Mom, this is Mickey Ahusaka. We work together."

"Pleasure to meet you, Mrs. McCabe," Mickey said, shaking his mom's hand.

"Oh please, call me Maggie. It's nice to meet you. Daniel doesn't have many friends." This set Mickey off, and he started laughing.

"Mom!" Daniel said with a groan, and his mom walked away giggling.

"Were you planning on waiting out here all day until I got back?" Daniel asked Mickey as they unloaded the truck.

"Nah, I was flying, keeping an eye on things, and saw you coming."

"Is everything okay?" he asked, while his mom was busy unpacking the food from the cooler into the icebox. Mickey told him how he warned off Viktor from Colleen the night before.

"Thanks, man, I owe you."

"No big." He shrugged. "I'm glad I was there. Viktor definitely had his eye on her."

"Where is she now, do you know?"

"She's at a church picnic with her family. I doubt any vampire will try anything on church property."

Daniel nodded in agreement and went back outside to close up his truck.

"I'm going to ask her out tomorrow," he told his friend, who had followed him.

Mickey stayed for a few minutes, but soon left so Daniel and his mom could get settled. The cabin was small. Daniel moved out of the one bedroom to the loft. Not quite a second floor, the loft was basically a small platform that extended out from the wall separating the living room from the bathroom. It cleared the ceiling by about four feet and overlooked the living room. The only access was a narrow ladder, which Daniel climbed up before tossing a pillow and sleeping bag onto the wood floor.

After one night of sleeping in the cramped space, Daniel decided that if they were going to stay in Havenwood Falls, they were going to need a bigger place.

The next morning, his mom drove into town with him. He showed her around the jobsite before she ventured off to explore, taking the truck in case she did any shopping. Daniel chuckled to himself as she drove away, because he knew there was no doubt that she would shop.

As noon approached, he found himself checking his watch more frequently. He'd normally be starving, his breakfast long worked off, but nerves kept his appetite at bay. What if Colleen rejected him? She could very possibly not be attracted to him or affected by the mating call at all. He had no idea what to expect since she was human. Finally, it was lunch time, and he dismissed the crew. Mickey clapped him on the back and wished him luck. Daniel needed it—he had no idea if Colleen would even be there.

Worry was replaced with nerves as he approached the bench and saw the back of her head, her blond hair a beacon in the shade of the tree. As he drew closer, he saw she was reading. He had already noted that was one of her hobbies, and he wanted to build her a bookcase. Hell, when they made a home together, he'd build her an entire library. *Way to put the cart in front of the horse, McCabe*, he cautioned himself and cleared his throat when he came to a stop in front of the bench.

"Is this seat taken?" he asked, and Colleen jerked her head up in surprise. When she saw him, she smiled a brilliant smile that was all dimples.

"It's all yours," she said and shifted over slightly to give him more room. She was wearing tan shorts that barely came to mid-thigh and showed off her gorgeous long toned legs. "I heard you left town?"

"Only to go pick up my mom and bring her here to visit."

She seemed relieved at that. Daniel noticed her posture soften a bit as she relaxed against the bench.

"I should warn you that you're quite the talk of the town, and the busybodies are already making matchmaking plans. You should have run while you had the chance." She teased, but he detected an edge to her tone. Was it jealousy?

"What if I already found a match?" he asked her, reaching out and brushing a stray curl away from her cheek. Her lips parted as he tucked the hair behind her ear and gently trailed his fingertips down her neck. Her eyes, deep brown with striations of amber, seemed to darken, and her eyelids lowered slightly.

"What do you mean?" Colleen whispered and grabbed his hand as he was pulling away. Everything snapped into focus the moment her fingers entwined with his. His hands were calloused and rough from work. They were darker than hers, tanned and freckled from hours spent in the sun. Hers were pale and soft, yet they fit together perfectly.

"I know you don't know me and that I'm not from around here, but I feel drawn to you—that we're connected somehow. I'm not going to ask if you feel it too, but I am going to ask if you'd be interested in going on a date?" He watched her closely to gauge her reaction, fully expecting her to retreat at some point, but she never did. Instead she squeezed his hand and smiled.

"Yes! I am very interested." Her smile was brighter than the sun and the most dazzling he had ever seen. Her natural beauty left him awestruck. The moment she said yes, a tightening in his chest released, and it was like he could breathe again. "And yes, I feel the connection, too."

Her cheeks flushed red when she said this, and she looked away. Her scent changed, heavy with pheromones and arousal, causing Daniel's nostrils to flare. Keeping himself in check was akin to wrestling an angry alligator. Desire coursed through his veins after the first inhale. She wanted him as much as he wanted her.

Colleen met his gaze again, and she slid closer, not breaking eye contact. When she sucked her lower lip in between her teeth, he was done. Closing the gap between them, he reached out with his free hand and cradled her cheek, his fingers sliding into her soft hair.

Closing her eyes, she leaned her head into his touch and released her lower lip, exhaling a soft sigh.

Initially, Daniel wanted to wait until they were on a date to kiss her, but the longer they touched and the closer they moved together, the more he felt his control slipping, like a tethered rope giving way thread by thread. Any concerns about her being human vanished, replaced with the overall sensation that this was right. Tilting her head slightly, he leaned in and captured her lips with his.

He'd heard others tell of their experience kissing their mate for the first time, and he'd thought they were exaggerating. Nothing could have prepared him for the earthquake that shook him from within— the force of two souls coming together and colliding. Not until they consummated would they be fully joined, and Daniel ached for that joining with every cell of his two beings.

A car horn blasted from nearby, breaking their connection, and they slowly separated. Colleen's cheeks were flushed a gorgeous pink, and her lips glistened from their kiss. Brown eyes, dark with lust, stared back at him. Drawing in a shaky breath, she moved back, slipping free of the gentle hold he had on her head.

"Wow," she whispered and touched her lips.

"Wow is right." He raised their joined hands and placed a kiss on the back of her hand. That's when he noticed the time.

"Crap, I'm going to be late."

"I'll walk with you," she announced and stood up with him, slipping her hand in his. It felt so natural, like something she had done countless times before.

"You don't have to work?"

"No, I had today off, but I came here hoping you'd show."

"I'm glad you did."

"Me too." She grinned and tugged on his arm, urging him to move. They walked hand in hand through the square and crossed Main Street at the crosswalk by the high school. Daniel told her how he and Mickey had found Herschel Ross. She gasped at the gory details and squeezed his hand when she thanked him for taking care of the man.

When they reached the entrance to the parking lot for Burger Bar, Daniel turned to say goodbye to Colleen, but she wanted to see the jobsite, so they continued on. Catcalls and whistles greeted them. Mickey stood in front of the crew with a big grin on his face.

"Way to go, boss!" he said and clapped Daniel on the shoulder. Colleen turned beet red at the attention.

"Yeah, yeah, whatever. Get to work," Daniel said with a laugh. The beginnings of the structure had been put in place, steel beams forming a grid. They had a tight schedule to meet the developer's deadline. Daniel explained this to Colleen as he took her inside the Airstream, which he had cleaned considerably in Herschel's absence, and showed her the blueprints and plans. Her face scrunched up like she had bitten into a lemon when she looked at the rendering.

"What's wrong?" he asked.

"It just looks so industrial. For the longest time before you started building, this empty dirt lot just sat here. Everything was barren. So many trees and shrubs were cleared to make room. I just wish the environment was taken into consideration."

"I agree with you."

"You do?" She looked up at him. They were side by side, leaning over the table, and he couldn't resist moving over and kissing the tip of her slightly upturned nose.

"I do. If I ever build something of my own, that's not part of someone else's design, I'm going to preserve as much of the natural environment as possible."

Smiling, she leaned into him, resting her head on his shoulder. "That's good."

Reluctantly, Daniel had to say goodbye. He needed to work, and he liked to be alongside his crew.

"Friday night. I'll pick you up for our date at say seven o'clock?"

"You know where I live?" Colleen asked.

Daniel, realizing his misstep quickly, recovered by laughing and smacking his forehead. "Of course not. That was going to be my next question."

Colleen found a piece of paper on the table and grabbed a pen.

She wrote down her address in perfect penmanship. She even drew a little map.

They left the trailer, and Daniel walked her to the edge of the Burger Bar parking lot, where she turned and, standing on tiptoes, pecked him on the cheek. This caused another chorus of catcalls and whistles, which made her blush again. Daniel watched her walk away, amazed at how easy she was to be around. Having overcome the obstacle of asking her out with success, the next hurdle was the actual date, and if their relationship progressed, that's when Daniel would face the biggest challenge of all: telling Colleen he occasionally turned into a mountain lion and that she was his fated mate.

CHAPTER 11

The walk home was a blur. Colleen basically floated down Main Street, ignoring anyone who called her name. She was too busy walking on clouds to stop. Her entire body hadn't stopped humming since Daniel kissed her. While she'd had her share of kisses, none of them compared.

As soon as the front screen door slammed closed, her mom appeared at the end of the hallway by the kitchen. She wore an apron over her dress and held a wooden spoon in one hand. "There you are! Sally has been calling here for you nonstop. She's getting on my last nerve."

As if on cue, the phone rang. Colleen dashed into the living room to answer it.

"Hello, Campbell residence."

"Colleen, you have some explaining to do!" Sally's shrill voice practically shattered her eardrum.

"What are you talking about?"

"Oh, don't be a ditz! I'm talking about that stud I saw you looking cozy with, strolling through town holding hands, and not one word to your best friend. How long have you been dating?"

"Um, well, we're not . . . not really. We're going on our first date on Friday."

"Gee whiz, Colleen! You all looked real comfortable with each other."

Colleen sighed and sat down on the sofa, curling her legs underneath and settling in to tell Sally everything: how it felt like she and Daniel were old friends, not new acquaintances, how he smelled better than anything, and that was when he was sweaty. She stopped short of telling her about the dreams. Those were a little too personal to share.

"You have it bad," Sally said with a note of longing.

"I think," Colleen peered around to make sure no one was listening before whispering into the phone, "I think Daniel's the one."

"Whoa."

"I know."

They chatted for a few more minutes, and Sally made her swear she would keep her updated. After she hung up the phone, Colleen remained on the sofa, lost deep in thought. She thought love at first sight was a myth reserved for fairy tales, but the way Daniel energized her, listened to her, and actually looked at her, and especially the way he kissed her, made her believe it was possible. Without even searching for him, she had found the perfect man.

Apparently keeping her newfound bliss a secret was easier said than done. The moment she sat down at the dinner table that night, her parents zeroed in on her.

"What?" she asked, the fork in her hand paused halfway to her mouth when she noticed her mom and dad looking at her.

"You look different," her mom answered.

Setting the fork down, Colleen patted at her hair, but everything felt in place. She smoothed her hands over her white sleeveless blouse, but all the buttons were secure. Picking up the cloth napkin from her lap, she dabbed at her mouth, but it came away clean. "Different how?"

"You're practically glowing," her dad said, which made her mom gasp.

"Colleen Morgan Campbell, are you pregnant?"

This question caused her brother to spray the milk he was drinking all over the freshly pressed tablecloth, and Kelly's mouth dropped open.

"What? No! Oh my word, how could you think that?" Colleen's bliss extinguished with that one question. Anger and embarrassment made her cheeks burn. "For your information, I'm still a virgin, Mother."

Poor David practically choked on this announcement.

"All right, rein it in," her dad said loudly. She looked over at him, and his cheeks were just as red. "Pumpkin, we were just making an observation."

This was one of those moments where Colleen realized she was outgrowing her childhood home. She was an adult, yet as long as she lived with her parents, they were going to treat her like a child. Even at work, while she was the assistant manager for the market, her dad still called her pumpkin. She didn't have the typical boss/employee relationship. Realizations like these made it hard to breathe, like the walls were closing in on her.

"I'm fine, Daddy. Can I be excused?"

He nodded, and she folded her napkin, setting it back on the table before grabbing her plate and bringing it into the kitchen. She scraped her half-eaten meal into the garbage and set the plate on the counter next to the sink. Movement caught her eye, and she looked out the window into the backyard. Dusk was setting in, and the shadows were long as the last bit of sunshine filtered through the trees. There, along the tree line, she saw it—a gorgeous mountain lion. Its amber eyes seemed to be locked on her. Instead of fear, she felt comfort with its presence. They stared at each other until she heard someone coming in from the dining room. Looking over her shoulder, she saw her sister.

"What are you doing?" Kelly asked.

"Come look at this mountain lion." Colleen waved her sister over to the window, but when they both peered through the screen, the big cat was gone. "Oh, too bad you didn't get to see it. He was beautiful."

"He?"

"Maybe, I don't know. I saw him in the backyard before one night when I couldn't sleep."

"Huh, I bet that's the animal that sprayed mom's bushes. Should we leave a saucer of cream out for it? Adopt a big cat as a family pet? Here kitty, kitty!" Kelly called.

"You're such a goof!" Colleen said with a laugh.

"What are you two carrying on about?" their dad interrupted.

"Colleen just saw a mountain lion in the backyard. We're going to adopt it."

His eyebrows rose with surprise, and then his expression grew serious. "You girls be careful. Wild animals shouldn't be approached. You let me know if you see this animal again, Colleen. I don't like the idea of a mountain lion sniffing around our house and getting comfortable."

"Oh, Daddy, relax. Remember, they were here first." With one final look out the window, Colleen left the kitchen. Grabbing her book from the table in the foyer, she turned on the porch light and slipped out the door to read on the porch. Within minutes she was lost within the pages of *Lord of the Flies*, her knuckles white from clenching the book so hard. The descent into cruelty and chaos as boys turned against each other and darkness and lightness of humanity fought for dominance kept her enthralled. So enthralled she didn't hear twigs breaking and leaves rustling as the mountain lion moved close and lay down between the bushes and porch, hidden from view.

CHAPTER 12

Throughout the week Daniel kept a nightly vigil on Colleen, needing to be close to her. Once her bedroom light turned off, he went back to the cabin. His mom actually joined him one night. The older she became, the less she needed to shift, but ever since she had arrived in Havenwood Falls, she told him the call to the wilderness was hard to resist. He enjoyed hunting alongside her. They took down a deer together and feasted on the fresh kill. During one of their many late-night conversations, she confessed she didn't want to go back to Fort Collins. She, too, had fallen under the spell of the small town.

So, while Daniel was busy running the Miller's Plaza job during the day, his mom was working with the local real estate agent on finding a larger place for them to live.

"But small enough for me to manage by myself when you and your mate settle down in your own home," she had said with a wink.

Finding a place to live was proving to be a challenge, though. Apparently Havenwood Falls had been experiencing a surge in population, resulting in a housing shortage. Ross Builders was the only construction company in town, and from what Daniel learned from Mickey, Herschel's unreliability and surly demeanor didn't make his phone ring for bids. After cleaning up the Airstream, Daniel imagined

Herschel's lack of organization had something to do with it too. He had unearthed a stack of unpaid invoices and several requests for bids in one of the kitchen cabinets.

In addition to keeping watch over Colleen at her house, he still met her for lunch in the square at what he considered their bench. They shared more kisses, held hands, and learned more about each other. Daniel opened up about his sister Katherine's death and his father's passing. He shared how they moved a lot when he was younger, so he didn't have close relationships. He learned that Colleen was the oldest of her siblings, and that in addition to reading, she liked to ride her bike and spend time with her friends, several of whom she had known since kindergarten. Their lives were significantly different, but they discovered they had things in common: conserving the environment and a love of cheeseburgers and Elvis Presley's music.

By the time Friday arrived, any apprehension Daniel had had over his first date with Colleen not going well was gone. Their lunches together had already forged a strong bond between them, enough that he could sense her emotions, like he was attuned to her specific frequency. Her scent was imprinted on his brain, too, and he could single her delicate floral fragrance out of a crowd, a heady mix of lilac and sunshine.

Instead of meeting Colleen for lunch that afternoon, Daniel stayed behind to finish paperwork and run some errands. He was in the Airstream, hunched over the table putting together a task list for the following week, when the door opened, and Herschel limped inside.

His face was almost back to normal. The swelling had gone down, leaving sickly yellow bruises behind. Several cuts had scabbed over, and one above his eye had required stitches. The black threads looked like an unruly extension of his eyebrow.

"McCabe, what are you doing here?" Herschel glanced around the trailer, taking in the changes with narrowed eyes. He licked his lips, and his fingers tapped against his thigh.

"Working, sir. The developer asked me to continue in your absence. Everything is on schedule."

"Good, good," he said, hobbling over to the table and running a shaking hand over the papers, but not really looking at anything specific. He licked his lips again, and beads of sweat dotted his receding hairline. That's when Daniel smelled it. Fear. No matter what species, it was an unmistakable stench of old sweat, sickening sweet endorphins, and ammonia. Daniel's lip curled up in response.

"Looks like you have everything in order."

"We have a good crew. Drew's cousin came on board, and Patty sent another laborer over, so we're up to eight now. They're all hard workers." Daniel set his pen down and leaned back, watching the nervous man in front of him with interest.

"It's a damn shame I have to shut it down," Herschel said, wandering away to peer out the narrow window that was over the small kitchen sink.

"What?" Daniel leaped to his feet. "Why?"

"I need to leave town . . . indefinitely. Circumstances being as they are, I won't be able to operate this business anymore. I'll be liquidating everything. Right now."

"You can't do that! The men—their jobs. The building needs to be finished." Daniel struggled to keep his anger in check. The coward had clearly screwed with someone, and the beating was a warning. Now he was going to run from his problems without any regard for anyone else. "How much do you owe? That's it, isn't it? You owe someone money?"

"Much worse than that." The color drained from Herschel's face, making his bruises stand out even more. "When you make a deal with the devil and he comes to collect . . ." He trailed off when there was a loud bang outside, causing him to spasm, and the smell of fear grew, filling the room. Daniel recognized the sound of the dumpster lid behind Burger Bar slamming shut.

"Give me the chance to buy you out. I'm committed to this job, this crew." Daniel spoke before thinking it through. He had a little bit of money saved up, but he doubted it was enough to buy a business. He had to try, though, and he knew if given the opportunity, he'd succeed.

Herschel approached the table and reached for the ledger, opening it up to the current balance of $6,457.86. He snatched up a pen and piece of scratch paper, then started writing down a figure. He included the amount in the bank account, the excavator, trailer, and an additional two thousand dollars on top for tools and other supplies. In total, in order to acquire a fully operational and established construction business in a town ripe for development, Daniel needed to come up with $19,657.86.

Fiddling with the edge of the paper, he thought through his options. He could ask his mom for a loan. She had her father's life insurance money. It might delay her buying a house, but he could build her one.

"Can I have until Monday to get this?" he asked.

Herschel licked his lips and ran a shaky hand over his balding head. "Yes, but no later than ten a.m. I need to be gone before noon."

"Deal." They shook hands, and Herschel quickly left the trailer.

For someone who wanted to disappear, running around town in broad daylight wasn't the best strategy, unless those looking for him operated under the cover of darkness. Herschel's comment about making a deal with the devil made Daniel shiver. If he came up with the money to buy Herschel out, he'd make the sure the notice of sale didn't have any hidden clauses.

After Herschel left, Daniel closed up the trailer and walked over to PPP Agency to pick up his paycheck. The arrangement Herschel had in place was that they managed all things personnel, from hiring to payroll. It was probably a good thing, as he probably would have screwed that up, too.

Patty Parker was sitting at her desk, and she greeted him with a big smile. "Daniel! How is everything going?"

"Good, except . . ." He spent the next few minutes filling Patty in on Herschel's visit. It was only fair to apprise her of the situation, in case Herschel disappeared and left the agency in a bind.

"Oh dear, that isn't good. Thank you for telling me. So, do you think you're able to buy him out?"

"I hope so. I want to."

"Well, I'm sure something can be worked out. Hold that thought."

She stared off into the distance with a blank expression. Daniel looked over his shoulder and out the window to see if there was anything happening on the street outside, but there wasn't anything of interest. Seconds later, Patty smiled and came back to earth. "Have a seat, Daniel. Elsmed will be here momentarily."

"What?"

She tapped her temple and grinned. "He's telepathic. I just projected my thoughts to him, and he responded. Sure beats the telephone sometimes."

Stunned at this revelation, Daniel did take a seat. Moments later, Elsmed Fairchild entered the agency. He was almost as tall as the doorway, and instead of wearing a tailored three-piece suit like the first time they met, he was decked out in hiking gear like he was going on a safari. His long blond hair was pulled back in a ponytail, and he carried a walking stick carved out of some sort of red wood in one hand.

"Let's go for a walk," he said to Daniel.

They walked down Main Street and past the high school. Once they reached Blackstone Road, Elsmed turned right, and they stayed on the shoulder of the road. To the right was the high school and elementary school, but the other side of the road, to the west, was undeveloped. Acres of relatively flat land lay out before him, with the mountains looming in the background.

"My sister had a vision of the future," Elsmed suddenly spoke, his first words to Daniel since they left the agency. "She saw a world taken over by technology. Cameras on every street corner, portable phones that people can make their own films with and take pictures. There is no privacy in the future. With that, it will become more difficult for the supernatural population to remain hidden." Elsmed paused, and he was suddenly speaking directly into Daniel's head. A tickling sensation, like fingers stroking his brain, sent shivers down his spine. *Your father's fears are rooted in truth. Humans, corporations, and governments will seek to either control or destroy us. They will fear us. You don't want to know what experiments they're conducting on aliens they have in custody.*

Just as quickly as Elsmed entered his thoughts and probed his innermost secrets, he was gone and picking up the conversation out loud. "My sister said more supernaturals will seek out Havenwood Falls. They will be drawn by the magic and will stay for protection from the threats of the outside world. We already have a housing shortage, and more homes will need to be built."

"There definitely is a need for more homes now. Did Patty tell you about Herschel?"

"She did, which is why I'm here. I have a proposal for you." From one of the large pockets on his tan field jacket, Elsmed withdrew a scroll. He unfurled it and presented the fibrous paper to Daniel. In flowing cursive, written in what appeared to be gold ink, was a proposal to enter a business agreement. Elsmed would be an investor in the construction business, just a silent partner. There were a few clauses. The Court occasionally had construction needs, and they preferred a supernatural to do the work.

"Explaining to a contractor why a building can't have any iron or needs secret underground passages can risk exposure. You'll be able to accommodate these special requests."

Daniel scratched the back of his head as he read the rest of the proposal. It all seemed straightforward.

"Good," Elsmed said, either picking up the thought directly or seeing it on Daniel's face. "Now, back to the housing shortage. I own all this property, and I've been reading up on these developments called subdivisions that are built around a golf course. I want one of those built here."

"A golf course?"

"Yes. Oddly enough, I've quite the affinity for the game."

"Okay, but if we're building a subdivision, I want to utilize the natural environment, conserve the local ecology as much as possible."

Elsmed beamed at him. It was an off-putting smile, more predatory than friendly, and his piercing blue eyes flared brighter. "What a marvelous idea! Being fae, I believe taking care of nature is a priority. I think we're going to get along famously.

"Now, there's another matter I want to discuss with you," Elsmed said as they started walking back toward town. His walking stick made a rhythmic *thunk-thunk* sound on the asphalt. "The Court likes each species to have a leader or representative for their kind. Someone who helps enforce the rules and such. Sheriff Kasun's wife is alpha of the Kasun wolf pack, and there's the Blaekthorn alpha. Each coven has their own leaders."

"And Jerome is the alpha of the mountain lions, right? That's why you sent him to welcome me to town."

"Well . . ." Elsmed paused with his hands crossed over the top of his walking stick and looked Daniel straight in the eyes. "He's not—not officially anyway. We approached him, and he declined. None of the other mountain lions are interested either. Your kind tend to keep to themselves."

"Why me? I'm an outsider, and young."

"Ah, you've made quite an impression in your first two weeks here. You're a natural leader, and I've been told youth will lead us to progress where some, myself included, are resistant to change."

"Natural leader? How do you know?"

Elsmed grinned again and started walking. "People talk and people watch. I listen and pay attention."

"Well. Let me think about that—one step at a time." Daniel's thoughts went to Colleen. She was his next step. He'd consider the leadership role later.

"Ah yes, your mate." Elsmed nodded, picking up on Daniel's thoughts—an unnerving ability Daniel probably would never get used to. *Don't think anything crazy around Elsmed.* At this, the fae laughed. *Crap, he heard that too.* "Don't worry about Miss Campbell. She's your mate, and while she's human, her subconscious recognizes you as such. When the time comes, approach the Court, and we'll assist with the reveal. There's a protocol in place for letting humans know about our existence."

Everything was falling into place. It almost seemed too easy, but after a lifetime spent moving, he was done, and he wasn't willing to turn down the opportunity to establish roots.

Since it was well past the end of the lunch break, Daniel brought Elsmed by the Miller's Plaza jobsite. His crew was already back to work, but they all came to a sudden stop when they saw him approach with Elsmed. Not all of them knew the fae's true nature or his role in town. He was seen as an eccentric man of wealth. He was a Fairchild, and the Fairchilds were one of the founding families.

"Hey, guys, I have something to run by you," Daniel called out, gesturing for the crew to join them. They gathered in a loose semicircle formation around him. "Herschel stopped by while you were at lunch," Daniel began and then filled them in on the opportunity to buy out the business and the proposal Elsmed had made. When he pulled the scroll from his back pocket, he almost dropped it, because it was no longer a scroll but rolled up regular paper, and the gold ink was now typewritten in black. He glanced over at Elsmed, and the fae winked at him, his blue eyes twinkling.

"I want to sign, but want your opinion first, since this is your livelihood, too."

"Do it, daddy-o!" Mickey shouted out, and the rest of the guys cheered in agreement.

"I know at least three other guys looking for work. They didn't want to work for Herschel, but they'll work for you, as they know you treat us well," Drew added.

"All right, I'll sign with you all as witnesses." Daniel took a deep breath and grabbed the pen from the breast pocket of his shirt. "I need someone's back."

Mickey volunteered and bent over so his back was straight. With a shaking hand, Daniel signed the contract and then handed the pen to Elsmed, who signed on the line next to Daniel's signature.

"It is done, Daniel McCabe. Now, let's go to the bank so we can finish this transaction."

After going around and shaking the hands of his crew, he and Elsmed left. Dizzy with excitement, Daniel barely remembered the walk to Havenwood Falls Savings and Loan. He registered the cool air from the air conditioning and the lemony scent of wood polish, right before Elsmed withdrew twenty thousand dollars and handed him the cash in large bills.

I'm glad you decided to stay in Havenwood Falls, Elsmed said directly into Daniel's mind. *Don't forget to get your tattoo upgraded to permanent resident status, and your mother needs one too.*

"I'm going to rename the business to McCabe Construction. Is that okay with you?" Daniel asked, out loud.

"Of course. It makes sense. Besides, I'm the silent investor. Do what you want."

That afternoon, Daniel tracked down Herschel, who was discreetly hiding out at the bottom of a bottle of whiskey in the Haven Saloon. Patty Parker had assisted Daniel in drafting the paperwork to buy the business off of Herschel, incorporating all the line items Herschel had listed out on the slip of scratch paper.

Daniel showed up at the saloon with the purchase agreement, notice of sale, and the cash. With the bartender as a witness, Herschel signed his business over without bothering to read anything, his eyes focused on the stack of cash. Before the ink was even dry, Herschel grabbed the money and bolted out the door.

"Hey! Are you going to pay your tab?" the bartender shouted after him, but Herschel was gone.

"Here." Daniel slapped a twenty-dollar bill down on the sticky bar. "Thanks for witnessing."

"Guess we won't be seeing old Hersch around anymore. Congratulations on your new business." The bartender poured them each a glass of Warded Whiskey, and he raised his shot glass for a toast.

"Just this one. I have a date tonight with a special gal," Daniel said when he reached for his glass.

"We'll make this a special toast then. To new beginnings."

"To new beginnings," Daniel repeated and tipped the glass back.

CHAPTER 13

*A*pproaching the front door, Daniel held a bouquet of flowers in one hand. He had handpicked the colorful array of wildflowers from the meadow behind his cabin, and his mom had tied a pale blue ribbon around the stems. Clearing his throat, he ran his free hand through his hair before knocking. Taking a step back, he waited for someone to answer, hoping it would be Colleen and that her parents had changed their minds about meeting him.

No such luck. Her father opened the door. He was shorter than Daniel, and he adjusted his glasses when he looked up. His brown hair was graying at the temples and thinning on top, and he wore khaki pants, a white button-down shirt, and a green tie. He took a few moments to examine Daniel as if sizing him up, his eyes pausing on the bouquet that was already beginning to wilt.

"Callum Campbell."

"Daniel McCabe." He shook the offered hand. Callum didn't invite Daniel in right away, but stood in the doorway, barring entrance.

"What are your intentions with my daughter?"

"Daddy!" Colleen admonished from somewhere behind her father.

"Callum, let the man in," said another woman's voice.

Callum Campbell stepped aside so Daniel could enter. Colleen

94

rushed forward and grabbed his hand. He swallowed hard when he saw her. She was a vision in curve-hugging black pedal pushers and a pale blue sleeveless top. A gold pendent sparkled around her long neck. Colleen tucked her arm through his and led him into the living room where the rest of Colleen's family waited.

The living room looked like the heart of the home and not one of those for decoration only. An oak coffee table had a bottom shelf covered with magazines. He recognized the recent cover of *Good Housekeeping*, as his mom had the same magazine at the cabin. Two low-sitting, deep purple chairs were positioned on one side of the coffee table, while a floral sofa with purple accent pillows was positioned on the other side, against the wall underneath the front picture window. Sheer ivory drapes covered both windows in the room, allowing for plenty of natural light. There were two matching end tables, and each had a lamp and one had a telephone.

A boy possessing the lanky limbs of adolescence sat in one of the chairs, and he regarded Daniel with cool blue eyes, sizing him up just like Colleen's father had. Two petite blondes, one an older version of Colleen and the other a younger version, sat on the sofa. Well, the younger one perched on the edge and grinned at Daniel. A giant family portrait hung above the fireplace mantle caught Daniel's eye.

"Colleen was seventeen when that was taken," the woman, who Daniel assumed was Colleen's mother, said when she stood up from where she was sitting on the sofa. She wore a pale-yellow dress with a full skirt that flared out the waist. A string of pearls decorated her neck.

"Daniel, this is my mom, Ellen."

"Pleased to meet you, Mrs. Campbell," he said and shook her hand.

"Colleen, why don't you put those flowers in some water? There's a vase in the hutch in the dining room." Ellen handed the bouquet to her daughter before turning her attention back on Daniel. "Please, sit down."

She directed him to the chair next to where Colleen's brother sat.

Callum followed them and continued on to sit down beside his wife on the sofa.

"Hello, I'm Daniel and you must be David?" he asked, extending his hand.

"Yeah, that's me." David shook his hand and at the same time snapped his gum. The loud crack sounded like a firecracker.

"I'm Kelly," Colleen's sister said with a giggle and waved from where she was sitting. "Do you have a younger brother?" she asked, eyeing him up and down.

"Kelly Marie!" Ellen scolded and shook her head. "Sorry Daniel, she's a little boy-crazy."

"A little?" David teased. "Try a lot crazy."

"Who's crazy?" Colleen asked, walking into the room. She set the flowers down in the middle of the coffee table before coming to stand beside Daniel. She placed her hand on his shoulder, and he felt himself lean into her touch. Her father noticed and scowled.

"Your sister is—never mind." Callum looked at Daniel. "So, what are your intentions with Colleen?" he asked again, crossing his arms over his chest.

"Daddy, cut it out," Colleen pleaded.

"It's okay, I get it," he told her. "I'll probably behave the same way when it's our daughter." As soon as he said it, Daniel realized his mistake, because the room went dead quiet with the exception of a surprised gasp from Colleen, and her hand tightened on his shoulder. "Er, I mean when I have a daughter."

An awkward silence filled the room, and Callum narrowed his eyes at Daniel. Ellen cleared her throat and changed the subject. "Colleen said you're taking her to dinner?"

Grateful for the change, he told them they were going to Burger Bar, and after, hopefully Colleen could show him around town a bit, since he was new to town. A few minutes later, the inquisition was over.

After closing the passenger door behind Colleen, Daniel walked around the front of his truck and slid into the driver's seat.

"Well, that was . . . terrible," he said, shaking his head and starting the engine.

Colleen threw her head back and laughed. "That was the most awkward . . . my poor father . . . the look on his face when you said 'our daughter.' Oh, my word." She paused and caught her breath, wiping a tear from the corner of her eye. "You certainly know how to make a first impression."

She dissolved into another bout of laughter, which was so infectious that Daniel joined in. Yeah, that was one heck of an impression. He hoped that was the only rough patch for the night. Unfortunately, it wasn't.

CHAPTER 14

While the date wasn't off to an auspicious start, the moment they were alone, things started to improve. Daniel drove them to Burger Bar, which was the place to go in town on a Friday night, if you were under thirty. Colleen was relieved he didn't take her to the Fallview Tavern & Grille, as it was kind of stuffy and the more refined, older crowd dined there. He parked off to the side and walked around to help her down. She placed her hand in his and stepped down onto the parking lot. Expecting him to let go once she was on her two feet, she was pleasantly surprised when he kept holding her hand. His touch was calming, and any concern she had been feeling about how it went with Daniel meeting her parents faded away.

Outside Burger Bar, all of the parking spots were taken where waitresses on roller skates came to take orders and brought trays of food right to the cars. She and Daniel walked past the rows of cars, and Daniel released her hand so he could open the door. He ushered her through, his hand on the small of her back, which sent a whole other feeling into her body that was the opposite of calm.

Inside, it was crowded and loud, and the delicious greasy smell of fresh French fries hung in the air. Music from the jukebox competed with the chatter of excited voices. Colleen noticed her friends, Peggy and Sally, sitting in one of the booths. She headed in that direction, with Daniel at her back. Peggy was facing them, and she grinned when she saw Colleen.

"I didn't know you girls were going to be here. What a nice surprise," Colleen said after introducing Daniel.

"Peggy needs help deciding on a china pattern, and decisions like those should be made over milkshakes," Sally said, taking a long suck on the straw sticking out of her chocolate shake. She looked Daniel up and down in the process.

"Oh, did you pick one?" Colleen asked Peggy.

"No. I like them all. This isn't an easy decision." She spun the catalogue that was open in the middle of the table toward Colleen. "Which one do you like?"

Colleen looked over the various patterns and descriptions in the catalogue. "I'm partial to the Noritake Edgewood pattern. The floral design that decorates the edge along with the silver trim is elegant and not too flashy."

With her input provided, Colleen and Daniel moved on to an empty table tucked in the corner.

"Your friends seem nice," Daniel said after they sat down.

"They are. We grew up together. How about you, do you have close friends?"

Daniel shrugged. "Not really. We moved around so much, it made making friends hard. Although since I've arrived in Havenwood Falls, Mickey Ahusaka has taken me under his wing."

"Mickey? He's a good guy. He was in the market this past weekend. I hope his brother is feeling better."

"What do you mean?"

Colleen filled Daniel in on Mickey's visit to the market, but how she saw his brother at Movies in the Park, seemingly fine.

"I'm sure he'd say something if his brother was ill." Daniel took a sip of his chocolate milkshake, and Colleen popped a French fry in her mouth. Just then "Whole Lotta Shakin' Going On" by Jerry Lee Lewis started playing on the jukebox, and people began to move into the middle of the makeshift dance area. Daniel suddenly stood up and held his hand out toward her.

"Come on, let's dance!"

"You dance?" she asked, raising her eyebrows in surprise, and placed her hand in his.

Daniel tugged gently on her arm, pulling her to her feet. They crossed the diner to the dance floor, and he surprised her when he spun around and effectively twirled her so they were in motion at the same time and perfectly in sync. He whirled her away from his body and then reeled her back in until they were face to face, their hands joined. They kicked their legs out and moved in unison, like they had rehearsed the dance for countless hours before. Daniel was graceful and moved so effortlessly that it took Colleen's breath away. She was grinning from ear to ear when he shimmied his hips like Elvis. The crowd surrounding the dance floor roared with approval, and she was laughing with sheer joy when he reeled her in again, causing her to land against his muscular chest. He lifted her and swung so her legs went to one side of his body, and he repeated this on the other side before dipping her low—so low she thought her hair was going to brush against the floor. The song ended, and Daniel slowly brought her back up to standing. She was panting slightly and couldn't take her eyes off of him.

The beginning notes of a ballad began to play, and they moved closer to each other. Daniel's arm slipped around her waist, his hand on her lower back, dangerously near her backside. Colleen looped her arms around his neck, relishing the press of her breasts against his chest. Elvis Presley's unmistakable croon filled the room. "I want you, I need you, I love you," Daniel mouthed the words along with the song, looking deep into her eyes the entire time. Their blue reminded her of the sky right after a storm moved through. Together they swayed in place, Daniel's hands burning through her clothes, setting her skin on fire. She imagined what it would feel like to be naked and flush against him. Her dreams involving Daniel had been vivid enough it wasn't difficult to imagine, especially with him so close to her now. He smelled incredible, earthy and spicy, natural . . . and familiar. Colleen leaned in and rested her head against his chest, letting out a contented sigh. She wanted to stay like this forever.

"Come on, I want to show you something," Daniel whispered in her ear. His lips brushed against the sensitive lobe, and she shivered in his arms.

"Is this where you turn from Mr. Wonderful to a cad?" she teased, winking at him, which caused him to throw his head back and laugh. It was a delightful, rich sound that sent vibrations through her body. She noticed the early traces of reddish brown stubble on the underside of his chin. Holding her hand, Daniel led her back to their table. She grabbed her purse, and he left more than enough money on the table to cover their bill. She waved goodbye to Sally and Peggy when they passed their table. Both girls were grinning like loons at her.

Once outside, Daniel led her in the opposite direction of his truck and around the back of the restaurant. Unlike the other night with Viktor, Colleen didn't hesitate. Something about Daniel made her feel safe. Dirt scraped under her heels, and she stumbled slightly. Daniel steadied her and moved so his hand was on the small of her back. They only had the distant glow of the lights from Burger Bar and moonlight to guide them, but Daniel moved with confidence, as if the darkness didn't exist.

They stopped in front of the door to the Airstream trailer, and Colleen briefly wondered if he *was* going to turn into a cad, recalling the sofa inside. She wasn't that kind of girl, no matter how badly she desired him.

Suddenly, there was movement behind them, and Colleen spun around to peer into the dark. A scrape of a flint followed by a flare illuminated a face before the Zippo lighter snapped closed, extinguishing the flame. The smoldering red dot of a cigarette gave the man's location away.

"Well, well, well, what do we have here?" A gravelly voice spoke, and a second man appeared, as if forming out of the shadows. Daniel moved in front of Colleen and stepped back, forcing her to be sandwiched between his body and the cool side of the trailer.

"Who are you?" Daniel asked, and she felt the tension coursing through him. He was practically vibrating with it.

"Depends. I could be your worst nightmare or your pal. It all hinges on information." The man with the gravelly voice moved closer, enabling Colleen to see his face clearer. Half of it was melted, disfigured by a horrific burn. The scars disappeared below the collar of his shirt, which stretched across his chest. He was a large man, his shoulders broad and square like he was carved out of granite. The man behind him, smoking, was even bigger, and he made an effective barrier blocking anyone's view of the trailer from Burger Bar.

"What kind of information?" Daniel asked, and Colleen noticed his hands had curled into fists. She sucked in a breath, bracing for a confrontation.

"I'm looking for Herschel."

Daniel's fists unfurled, and Colleen exhaled, slumping against the trailer, letting it support her weight, as her knees had turned to Jell-O.

"He's in the wind. He sold me his business and skipped town. Claimed the devil was after him."

Gravel man laughed, and it was a horrible sound, like boulders being ground against each other.

"That's not the answer I'm looking for." He moved closer. "What about you, sweetheart, do you know where Herschel is?"

The moment the man spoke to her, Daniel tensed up again. She placed a hand against his back, a silent plea for him to stay where he was. Menace choked the air, and Daniel was her shield. She didn't like the way the man's dark eyes glittered when they focused on her. He licked his lips and smiled, but only half of his mouth worked, the side that hadn't melted like wax. The lopsided leer left her more unsettled. While Daniel was muscular and in shape, the two men were giants in comparison. She didn't want to answer him, to open up a conversation, but she didn't want to anger him by not responding either, so she shook her head.

"That's a damn shame," he said to Daniel. "You see, Herschel owes me money. A lot of money. He wagered his business in a poker game. I came to collect. Only now the business is yours." He paused and ran a hand over his ruined face. "A pretty little morsel like your girl will be a decent consolation prize, though."

Without warning, a giant fist was heading toward Daniel's face. Colleen flinched, preparing for the impact, but before she could blink, Daniel had spun out of the way, moving Colleen with him and out of harm's way. He roared, an animalistic sound that reverberated down her spine, and then he was leaping through the air. Convinced it was a trick of the poor lighting, Colleen dismissed what she thought she saw because it looked like Daniel's hands had turned into paws tipped with sharp, pointy claws. The man cried out and toppled backward underneath Daniel's weight. Daniel raised his head and hissed, actually hissed at the smoking man, who tossed his cigarette to the side and began to advance. Another animalistic growl came from behind the smoking man, causing him to turn around and look.

Colleen recognized DJ Brewster standing at the edge of Burger Bar's parking lot. She hadn't seen much of him since they graduated high school. He stood in a fighter's pose, but his eyes captured her attention. They seemed to glow.

A piercing cry joined the other sounds around her, and she looked up to see a hawk circling overhead before it flew off with an incredible burst of speed. Soon Daniel and DJ were engaged in an all-out rumble with the two strangers. Every time a fist landed on Daniel's body, she flinched. He took a particularly hard hit and went down. He wasn't moving, and Colleen ran forward, not caring about the fight going on around her. Before she could reach Daniel, the man with the melted face had her upper arm in a vise-like grip. She struggled to free herself, but it only made him laugh.

"Feisty little bird, aren't you?" He started dragging her away from Daniel. One of her shoes slipped off, and the gravel tore at the skin on her foot.

"Stop! You're hurting me!" she cried out.

Something flashed in her peripheral vision, and she turned to see Daniel getting up into a crouch. Then, before her eyes, he transformed. His body bent and folded in the most unnatural manner, accompanied by loud cracking and popping sounds. With a triumphant howl, a mountain lion stood among bits of shredded clothing, in Daniel's place. She was vaguely aware of her arm being released, and she heard the man back away, but her eyes were fixated on the familiar, magnificent cat before her. She recognized him. This was the mountain lion she had seen in her backyard.

He was a blur of golden fur as he ran past and gave chase, pursuing the man who had threatened her. Within seconds, the man was down on the ground, pinned with a mouthful of fangs attached to his throat. DJ had taken control of the other man and had him pressed face-first into the dirt. This was how Sheriff Kasun found them when he arrived a few minutes later. His truck came to a stop, and he leapt out. Colleen was surprised to see Mickey get out from the passenger side. He was wearing jeans that were a little too big on him, and that was it—no shoes or shirt. Mickey's muscles rippled with movement, and he caught her looking. Embarrassed, she turned away just in time to watch Daniel transform back into his human form.

She had never seen a man completely naked before, and her pulse accelerated, her mouth went dry, and her lower extremities began to tingle when she took in Daniel's body. She was frozen in place and couldn't stop staring.

Sheriff Kasun snapped handcuffs on the melted-faced man and hauled him to his feet. The sheriff manhandled him like the man weighed less than one hundred pounds. Mickey joined Daniel and handed him an Army green blanket, which he wrapped around his waist. Their eyes locked, and in an instant, Daniel was there. He cupped her face, his hands warm against her cheeks, and he drew her in, crushing his lips against hers. With a moan, she reciprocated, feeding off of his urgency.

When they separated, there was still a wildness about him. His nostrils flared slightly, and his thick hair, usually smoothed back, stuck up in all directions.

"Are you okay?" he asked, his hands exploring her arm that the man had gripped. His nostrils flared again as his eyes zeroed in on her bleeding foot. The scrapes were minor, but not to Daniel. Heedless of the blanket loosely knotted around his waist, he scooped her up in his arms.

"Daniel, put me down!" she protested.

"No. You're hurt. Let me take care of you." His voice was rough. "I'll always take care of you."

He carried her over to the sheriff's truck and set her down on the hood. After examining her foot, he gently brushed the dirt off. He wedged himself between her legs, facing her, eyeing her.

"What?" she asked.

"You're not in hysterics or running away screaming. Aren't you afraid of me? You shouldn't have seen that."

Colleen took a few minutes to assess and gather her thoughts, since the shock was beginning to wear off. Was she surprised? Yes, but not scared. Daniel protected her. With him, she was safe.

"Would you have ever told me what you are?"

"Eventually. My kind haven't had it easy. It would have been difficult for me to disclose, but if we got serious, I wouldn't keep it from you."

"Your kind. So, there are more of you?" He nodded. "That's an awful lot of woulds and ifs," she said, tracing a finger along his chest, enjoying the silky feel of his skin and the way his muscles jumped under her touch.

"Do you want for there to be an us?" Daniel asked, cocking an eyebrow. He moved in closer, his hands resting on top of her thighs.

"Will you tell me everything?"

"Yes. Whatever you want. I am yours."

THEY FOLLOWED Sheriff Kasun back to the station. Both men were handcuffed and secure in the back of his truck. Mickey and DJ followed behind in DJ's car. All of them were required to give their statements. Miraculously, for being so close to Burger Bar, a crowd hadn't gathered, and there weren't other witnesses to the fight. Colleen thought for sure her cries had been heard.

It didn't take long for her father to rush into the station. He wore a pajama top and a wrinkled pair of khaki pants. He had the bleary eyes of someone who had been rudely woken from a deep sleep.

"Pumpkin! Are you okay? Sheriff Kasun said you were involved in an altercation."

"I'm fine, Daddy. Daniel protected me."

"Oh, thank goodness." He sunk down in the chair next to her. "Where is Daniel?"

"Giving his statement. Apparently, those are the same men who beat up Mr. Ross."

"Anyone we know?"

Colleen shook her head. "Never saw them before, and their faces aren't ones I'd forget." She shuddered, remembering the lopsided leer.

The front door to the station opened again, and they both looked to see who had come in.

"I wonder what Elsmed Fairchild is doing here this late at night?" Callum asked.

"Daniel called him. He told me that Mr. Fairchild is his silent partner. Daniel bought Ross Builders."

"Well, I'll be. Guess he's going to be sticking around then, huh?" He gave her a knowing look. She just blushed and grinned in response.

CHAPTER 15

*E*lsmed entered the small room where Daniel sat across from Sheriff Kasun. Now that the two gangsters who had followed Herschel back from Grand Junction were locked up in the holding cell, Daniel had to face the consequences of his actions. He had shifted in front of a human.

"Colleen is my mate. When she was threatened, I lost control."

"You're lucky Mickey found me just in time. Had we arrived ten seconds later, you would be facing a murder charge. I know how close you were to ripping that man's throat out."

Daniel hung his head, acknowledging it was true. His fangs had punctured skin, and when the blood welled against his tongue, the killing instinct kicked in. How easy and satisfying it would have been to rip that man's throat out. To punish him for hurting his mate. *His mate.* "What's going to happen to Colleen, now that she knows?"

Elsmed fielded this question. "It's up to her. I'll give her the option of wiping her memory. She'll forget tonight's events ever happened. I can even make her forget you. You haven't fully consummated the mating bond, so the symptoms for her will lessen in time."

Daniel's palms grew sweaty at the idea of Colleen forgetting him. Now that he'd met his mate—had forged a connection with her—his inner mountain lion would slowly go feral. The longer he denied himself the mating bond, the deeper the descent into madness. The ache in his chest he felt when he was away from Colleen would become an unbearable pain. He'd heard of other shifters ending their lives to end the suffering.

"It's her choice, though. What if she refuses and doesn't want to have her memories altered?"

"Then you're a lucky man," the sheriff answered. "I'll go bring her into my office," he said to Elsmed.

Moments later, Daniel was alone in the room with his thoughts. Panic threatened to take control. What if she decided he wasn't worth it? What if she didn't feel the same way about him? He fought the urge to burst into the sheriff's office and abscond with Colleen—force her to accept him as her mate.

The door opened, and he looked up, hoping to see the petite blonde, but saw Mickey instead. He was followed into the room by DJ Brewster, whom he hadn't met before that night.

"Thanks for your help," he said to DJ. "I owe you one."

"My grandfather owed you, so we can call us even."

"Grandfather?" Daniel looked at the other mountain lion shifter, and he did seem familiar. There was something about his straight nose and thick, dark eyebrows, even his scent. "Wait a minute, is Jerome your grandfather?"

"He is, and he told me about our family's history. Guess I might not be here if not for your grandfather. When you're ready, I'll introduce you to the other mountain lion shifters. They're anxious to meet you."

"Yeah, well, I might be feral soon," Daniel said, rubbing the tightness in his chest. It had been growing worse the longer he sat in the confined space. The longer he was away from his mate.

"Have some faith, daddy-o." Mickey clapped him on the shoulder as he sat down next to him. "I hope to be so lucky someday to have a woman look at me like Colleen looks at you. Even from twenty-five feet in the air, I could see it."

"I hope you're right."

EPILOGUE

THREE YEARS LATER—SEPTEMBER 1960

"So, what do you think, Mrs. McCabe?" Daniel asked, nuzzling his wife's neck right above the faint scar from his mark. He loved the reaction this elicited. It never failed that goose bumps erupted over her entire body when he brushed against the sensitive area. He stood behind her, his arms wrapped around her waist and his hands cradling her belly that was just beginning to swell. They were standing at the entrance to the recently completed Creekwood Estates Country Club, which was built at the top of a small hill. Green grass, wildflowers, and trees stretched out before them on one of the most natural golf courses in the country. No chemicals were used to maintain the greens. A herd of antelope grazed by the ninth hole. Daniel tracked their movement, his inner cat's interest piqued. Streets dotted with new homes had been built around the natural landscape, some with dramatic curves around existing boulders. Phase One of Creekwood Estates was complete. The grand opening for the country club was scheduled for the following day.

"Oh, Daniel. It's beautiful," Colleen replied and leaned back against him, placing her hands on top of his and giving them a squeeze. "I see you used my idea of utilizing the natural springs for irrigation."

"I sure did, and it saved at least ten thousand dollars off the estimate from the landscape architect. Thanks to my brilliant mate." He kissed the top of her head. "Come on, are you ready to see the house?"

He stepped away and held out his hand. She entwined her fingers through his, and they walked hand in hand across the giant flagstone patio to the wide French doors that led to the club.

Inside it was all dark wood and rich tapestries in shades of green, brown, and gold. Vaulted ceilings with exposed beams loomed overhead. They crossed a dance floor, the parquet floors so brand new, they weren't marked by a single scratch. Then they walked through the dining room, which consisted of twenty tables, all with high-backed upholstered chairs. An enormous gold chandelier was suspended from the ceiling. A large stone fireplace took up one wall. A brown leather sofa and two green velvet lounge chairs were positioned in front. Along the other wall the bar was set up—a stone base with a long top made out of a red oak tree that had been uprooted during a blizzard the year before. Shelves built into the wall behind the bar were stocked with only top-shelf liquor. At the front of the club, there was the membership office, a banquet room, and the pro shop. When they stepped out front, twelve brand new golf carts were parked in a row along the curb of the curved driveway.

Their house was less than a block away, and soon they were walking up the driveway to their new split-level home. A large mottled-gray stone chimney jutted up from the center, and the bottom level of the house was built out of the same stone, where the second level had wood siding. Wide windows spanned the front of the house. Daniel and Colleen both wanted the view of the mountains to be unrestricted. Upon entering, a wide flight of stairs led them up to the second level and another set of stairs led to the first floor. They went upstairs, where several of the mountain lion shifters were moving furniture in the living room. A fireplace took up the center of this floor and would provide heat for the entire level. DJ, Daniel's beta, grinned when they entered the kitchen. All of the appliances were top-of-the-line General Electric and a butterscotch brown that blended in with the stained pine cabinets.

"Is it ready?" Daniel asked, and DJ nodded.

"What's ready?" Colleen peered up at him.

"You'll see." He leaned down and kissed the tip of her nose.

Leading Colleen down the carpeted hallway where the bedrooms were located, he pulled her into the smallest one at the end, and it was like stepping into a bowl of sunshine.

"Oh, Danny!" she gasped and twirled around in the center of the room, taking everything in. The walls were painted a daffodil yellow, and the trim was white. A natural wood crib sat against the wall underneath a bay of windows. A matching wood dresser was against the wall to the right, in between the door and closet. A rocking chair was placed next to the crib with a blanket knitted by Colleen's mom draped over the back. Pink, blue, yellow, and green yarn had been used to make it, since they wouldn't know the sex of their first child until he or she was born. A mobile extended over the crib, each item an animal: lion, tiger, bear, monkey, horse, pig, cow, and a special-order item Daniel requested—a mountain lion. Several pillows and stuffed animals were propped up along the sides of the crib. A mural of Winnie the Pooh sitting with his paw in a jar of honey had been painted on the wall to the left.

"It's perfect!" she announced and walked into his arms.

She slid her hands into the back pockets of his Levi's and hummed with contentment. The new fullness of her breasts pressed against his chest, and his hands slid down her sides, coming to a stop on her fuller hips. He loved her new curves and that she carried their child. He nuzzled her neck again, moving her hair aside with his nose so he could gain access to bare skin. Lilac and sunshine filled his nose, and he inhaled deeply before placing soft kisses along her neck. Sucking gently on her mark made her moan and shift closer, squeezing his ass through the thick denim. It never got old, how quickly they responded to each other.

Since the first night they truly bonded and he claimed her completely, they had been in sync. One of his favorite things to do was to listen to their heartbeats. They beat as one.

"Honey, we're in a house full of people and in our child's nursery. We'll get frisky later, when we're alone," Colleen murmured against his chest.

"You're right. We're definitely finishing this later," he whispered in her ear and felt her body quiver against his, her scent becoming muskier with desire.

"You're bad," she scolded breathlessly and swatted his chest when she backed away. "Let's go look at the rest of the house."

They finished exploring, and as they walked back to the country club, where their truck was parked, they started their debate on baby names. Since Colleen first found out she was pregnant, she had been obsessing over names. With four months left until their baby was due, she was feeling the pressure to pick out a name.

"How about Petunia if we have a girl?" Daniel suggested, and Colleen scowled.

"That's an awful name."

"Okay, what about boys' names? I've always been partial to Michael."

Colleen stopped in the middle of the newly paved street and tilted her head to the side, something he had learned early on in their relationship meant she was thinking the idea over, weighing the pros and the cons.

"Michael McCabe. I like it." She rubbed her belly, which was just beginning to test the confines of her shirt.

Looping her arm through his, they continued walking. The streets of Creekwood Estates were quiet now, but all of the homes of Phase One had already sold out, and planning for Phase Two was in the beginning stages. Daniel looked around at the life he was building for himself, for others, and for his growing family. His children would grow up playing on these streets, safe and unafraid of being singled out for being different. Looking down at his beautiful bride, glowing with pregnancy,

Daniel was so glad he chose to accept her, that he chose love over hate.

~

We hope you enjoyed this story in the Legends of Havenwood Falls series featuring a variety of supernatural creatures. The series is a collaborative effort by multiple authors.

Books by E.J. Fechenda in the Havenwood Falls world:
Fate, Love & Loyalty
Fata Morgana
Fated Beginnings
Stray With Me
Forever Loyal
Sun & Moon Academy Book One: Fall Semester
Sun & Moon Academy Book Two: Spring Semester

Books in the historical Legends of Havenwood Falls series:

Lost in Time by Tish Thawer
Dawn of the Witch Hunters by Morgan Wylie
Redemption's End by Eric R. Asher
Trapped Within a Wish by Brynn Myers
Blood and Damnation by Belinda Boring
Fated Beginnings by E.J. Fechenda
Emeline by Katie M. John
Released From a Curse by Brynn Myers
A Pack of Lies by Kallie Ross
Kiss the Ashes by Desiree Lafawn
Hidden Truths by Colleen Nye
Wrath and Retribution by Belinda Boring
Changing Fate by Char Webster
Rise of the Witch Hunters by Morgan Wylie
The Drowning Bride by Seven Jane

Also try the main Havenwood Falls series; the YA line, Havenwood Falls High; the darker, sexier side of town, Havenwood Falls Sin & Silk; and the local supernatural college, Sun & Moon Academy.

Stay up to date at www.HavenwoodFalls.com

Subscribe to our reader group and receive free stories and more!

ABOUT THE AUTHOR

E.J. Fechenda has lived in Philadelphia and Phoenix, and now calls Portland, Maine, home. She is the Amazon bestselling author of the New Mafia Trilogy and in addition to working on the Ghost Stories Trilogy, she's a contributing author for the Havenwood Falls series. She has a degree in Journalism from Temple University, and her short stories have been published in *Suspense Magazine* and several anthologies. E.J. is a member of the Maine Writers and Publishers Alliance.

You can find her on the internet here:

Facebook: https://www.facebook.com/EJFechendaAuthor

Twitter @ebusjaneus (https://twitter.com/ebusjaneus)

Tumblr: http://ejfechenda.tumblr.com/

ACKNOWLEDGMENTS

A year has passed since my journey with Havenwood Falls began, and what an epic adventure it has been. I've met so many incredible authors and readers. We support each other, are silly together, and have built an amazing world together. My heart is full of love for you all. Kristie, I don't know how you keep everything straight and keep us authors on task. You are truly brilliant with a little bit of evil mastermind thrown into the mix. Thank you for taking a chance on me.

Every time I work on a new project, I lose myself a bit and withdraw to the "writing cave." My social life is impacted as most weekend nights are spent writing. To my family, especially the hubs, and friends who tolerate this and understand, I appreciate you more than you know and we will make up for lost time—promise!

~A Havenwood Falls New Adult Novella~

HAVENWOOD FALLS

FATE, LOVE, & LOYALTY

E.J. FECHENDA

Fate, Love & Loyalty (A Havenwood Falls Novella) by E.J. Fechenda

Aster McCabe couldn't be happier with her job managing Coffee Haven and baking blueberry scones the whole town raves about, especially her sweet and sexy boyfriend Patrick. She loves her simple, small-town life in Havenwood Falls. At least, until her sister suddenly shows up with trouble not far behind.

The sisters' relationship has always been volatile, especially with the pressure of being the Alpha's daughters and the expectation to be perfect. Reeve never failed in that department, and Aster grew up in the shadows of her sister's success. But when Reeve left for college, Aster blossomed. So she's dealt a painful blow the moment her sister walks in the door and meets Patrick—a mountain lion's call to its mate couldn't be any more obvious. Neither can it be controlled or refused.

When an unstable Alpha from another den claims Reeve as his mate, Aster, bitter over the recent betrayal, practically draws the guy a map to Reeve's location, unknowingly putting her entire family and den in danger. Aster must figure out how to right her wrong and save her family. But loyalty and love are further tested when a stranger appears with the potential to forever change Aster's fate.

FATE, LOVE & LOYALTY

AN EXCERPT

*T*he bell above the front door chimed, and Aster McCabe looked up from the espresso machine, anticipating her boyfriend since she'd been counting down the minutes all morning. They were going away to celebrate their six-month anniversary with a long overdue trip to her family's cabin located in a remote area in the mountains. There they'd be able to shift and run and hunt together, away from the watchful eyes of the community. With Patrick being new to the den and new to Havenwood Falls, there were some who viewed his attachment to Aster as more of a strategic political move. Being the alpha's daughter placed Aster and anyone she became involved with under more scrutiny—a fact that she hated. She always felt she was being held to a higher standard than the other members of their den, and her perfect sister, Reeve, had raised the standards even higher. At the thought of her sister, Aster scowled. The last time Reeve had been home was for Christmas, right before Patrick had shown up in town, and they'd fought constantly.

Instead of Patrick, Aster's boss, Willow Fairchild, walked in cradling her swollen belly—the reason why she'd been showing up later and later for work. A gust of wind followed her in, carrying the sweet fragrance from catalpa trees that were in full bloom. The town square across the street was home to several of these towering trees, which had more fluffy white blossoms than leaves.

"How are you feeling?" Aster asked, deftly steaming milk without even looking at the machine.

"Good. Tired. The baby kicked up a storm last night." Willow eased into a chair at one of the few empty tables near the front counter.

"I can cancel my weekend away if you're not up to running the shop," Aster offered as she handed a latte to a waiting customer.

"No, no. You and Patrick have been planning this. I'll be fine, and Paisley is able to work some extra hours." Willow dismissed Aster with a wave of her hand before resting it back on top of her baby bump. With her white-blonde hair and pixie features, Willow looked barely old enough to be pregnant. While her fae heritage gifted her with a youthful appearance, she was really six years older than Aster. After Aster graduated from college in December, Willow promoted her to manager—a timely decision, since Willow found out a month later that she was pregnant.

Shadows under Willow's eyes, more noticeable because of her porcelain skin, made Aster worry. What if she left and something bad happened? Willow had become more like the sister she wanted, and Aster suddenly felt guilty about leaving. Was it selfish of her to go? She attempted to shrug off the negative thoughts, but it was too late. Willow had already received them. It was hard to hide anything from her boss, one of Havenwood Falls' most powerful empaths. She sensed emotions from miles away.

"Stop it, Aster," Willow said. "You worry too much about what other people think. You need to get out of here and let loose—it will do you some good."

Aster smiled and smoothed her apron, wiping at a clump of flour from a batch of her blueberry scones that won Best of Havenwood Falls two years in a row. Streaks of white powder stood out against the black fabric. "I know."

Willow's command was easier said than done. Having grown up in Reeve's shadow, Aster had years of feeling insecure holding her back.

Reeve had moved to Denver and had been gone for more than six years, but the comparisons never stopped. Reeve was high school class valedictorian, she was Miss Teen Havenwood Falls, and she practically walked on water. Guys of all species salivated in her wake. Back then, Aster had been an awkward teenager, and puberty hadn't been kind. All knobby knees and elbows with carrot-orange hair that stuck out in a riot of uncontrollable curls, she was a far cry from beautiful Reeve. She was even envious that her sister was able to leave Havenwood Falls to move to the city, where she lived a glamorous life. Of course, the Court of the Sun and the Moon, the governing body for supes in town, made an exception for her and lifted the spell that usually made other supes and humans forget their time spent in Havenwood Falls.

"You're doing it again." Willow's voice broke through Aster's thoughts. "Have you heard from Reeve?"

"Not lately. She's probably busy planning some extravagant event for some celebrity." Aster turned around to open the oven door. Heat blasted her skin, and the sweet aroma of blueberries and cinnamon assaulted her nostrils. She grabbed an oven mitt and pulled out a tray of golden-brown scones, setting them on the marble counter to cool. She loved the old-fashioned counter and that she didn't have to worry about using a cooling rack or hot pad.

"Aster, you have carved out your own life here and landed an awesome job with the coolest boss ever. Oh, and you have a hot piece of man meat. Who knows, soon you could be sporting one of these." Willow patted her baby bump dramatically, making Aster laugh.

"No! Hell no! I'm not ready for that." Aster shook her head in denial, her ponytail swishing along her back with the movement. Her once carrot-orange hair had darkened to a light auburn, and the longer she grew it, the more the curls relaxed. These days she had grown to appreciate her locks, but had to keep them pulled back. No one appreciated hair in their scones. While she disagreed with Willow on babies, she did agree with her about having an awesome job.

Aster surveyed the shop, taking a moment to admire all of her hard work over the past year. Paintings from local artists hung on the red brick walls, adding color to the space. At Aster's suggestion, Willow had added flower boxes to the large front picture window, and the wildflowers that bloomed were a cheerful greeting to anyone walking by outside. Several hanging plants inside, along with Willow's crystal collection, added a quirky vibe. Overall, the effect was relaxing and inviting. Combined with the good coffee and food, Coffee Haven was a favorite among locals and visitors.

"Well, it's going to happen one of these days, because you're a catch. Why do you think eighty-five percent of our customers are male?" Willow winked, because at that moment Patrick walked in the door. "And all of them are hot for you. Feelings . . . I pick up on these things, you know," she said and tapped her temple.

"Who's hot for you, besides me?" Patrick said with a growl. He stalked across the shop and around the counter, pulling Aster into his arms. She sank into his warmth and breathed in his musk. He rubbed his cheeks against her hair, an instinctual way of marking her with his scent. She tilted her head up, and he slanted his mouth over hers, sending the message to any male in the coffee shop that she was taken. This sent a shiver through her, though she never would have admitted the whole display of male dominance turned her on. Of course, Willow picked up on it and started to giggle. Aster flipped her off behind Patrick's back, which made Willow laugh even harder.

"You ready to go, babe?" Patrick asked when they separated.

"Yes," she responded breathlessly. "My bag is upstairs."

One of the perks of being manager of the coffee shop was the apartment upstairs, which Willow rented to her at a reduced rate, since having a mountain lion shifter living upstairs was added security. Aster untied her apron and tossed it in the hamper under the sink.

Just as they were preparing to leave, the bell above the door chimed. Aster turned to see who was coming in and froze in place. *What the hell was Reeve doing here?* There her sister stood, wearing simple jeans and a black T-shirt, but still managing to showcase every curve. Her hair looked like she had just had it professionally styled; auburn waves framed her heart-shaped face. While Aster was momentarily stunned, Patrick was not, and she watched in disbelief as he prowled toward Reeve.

"Patrick?" Aster called, and she reached for his arm, but he shrugged her off. "Patrick!" she said louder, and he looked back at her briefly with a dazed look in his eyes.

He blinked once, slowly, before focusing on Reeve again. Aster stared in disbelief as she noticed Reeve's dreamy expression and how her sister tracked Patrick's every move. Then she realized what was happening, and her stomach dropped to her toes. She'd seen this before, when their brother Braden met his wife, Kaitlyn.

"Oh, shit," Willow said from behind the counter, and Aster looked at her. "I'm so sorry, honey." Her bright blue eyes shone with sympathy.

Willow's confirmation hit Aster like a punch in the gut, and she bent over as if in physical pain. She couldn't breathe and couldn't process what was happening. Reeve wasn't even supposed to be there in the first place.

"Unbelievable!" she screamed. "You always get everything. Why?"

She couldn't bear to look at them anymore as they scented each other and began touching every inch of exposed skin, oblivious to anyone else around them. With a sob, Aster stormed out through the back of the shop. As soon as she was in the alley behind Coffee Haven, she stripped off her clothes, shifted into her cat form, and took off for the woods on the outskirts of town. She didn't care that running through town as a mountain lion was frowned upon or that there would be consequences. All she cared about was running far away from her sister before she did something stupid, like gouge her eyes out with her claws . . . or kill her.

For Reeve McCabe, meeting her true mate couldn't have come at a worst time. She wanted to fight it, but was powerless against the attraction. She felt inexplicably drawn to the handsome stranger in the coffee shop, and he became her only focus. She smelled her sister's scent all over him, and it made her want to pounce on him to claim him right then and there. Aster. The only reason she stopped by the coffee shop to begin with. She broke away from her mate's gaze when her sister cried out and winced when she saw the hurt on Aster's flushed face, her red cheeks stained with tears. When Aster took off, Reeve ran after her.

She called out for Aster to come back, but by the time she reached the alley, Aster was gone, her clothes a discarded heap on the pavement. Reeve started to call her cat forward so she could pursue her sister, but her cat had nothing but mating on her mind and refused to cooperate. She was unable to leave her mate. She didn't even know his name or where he came from, but that didn't matter. Now that they'd crossed paths, she knew she'd never stray far from his side.

She had come to tell Aster she was home for an indefinite amount of time. Life had gone sideways in Denver, and she needed the security, the protection, of the den and her family. Trouble had followed Reeve lately, and sadness weighed heavy on her heart when she realized the source of her sister's anguish. Her mate was Aster's boyfriend. Shit. Without even meaning to, she had once again caused her sister pain. With a sigh, Reeve picked up her sister's clothes and folded them. She brought them inside and left them in a neat stack on top of a cardboard box before returning to her mate.

"I feel just as shitty, too. Aster doesn't deserve this. She's a good person. I've seen you in the pictures she has in her apartment. You're Reeve?" her mate asked in a deep voice that echoed within her soul. He brushed a tear off of her cheek before his hands came to rest on her hips, and she felt the strength they possessed. His eyes were a warm brown, framed with thick lashes. His light brown hair was long on top and tousled. A straight nose brought her attention to his full lips.

"Yes," she replied and stepped closer so their bodies were a breath apart. "And you are?" His heart pounded a strong, steady beat, and she was shocked to discover her heartbeat had already aligned with his.

"Patrick O'Shea." A hand left her hip and ghosted up her side, lightly brushing against her right breast before cupping her cheek. She leaned into his touch and purred. All thoughts of anything except Patrick disappeared when he touched her. She knew they had an audience in the coffee shop, but she didn't care. The instinct to fully mate with Patrick clouded her brain. "Please tell me you have your own place, because I'm staying with my parents."

Patrick smiled, his canines already grown longer, and his eyes flashed golden. "I do. Let's go."

They quickly left Coffee Haven, a boatload of pheromones following them out the door.

Patrick lived in Havenwood Village, an apartment complex located a block away from downtown Main Street. At the speed they ran, they reached his apartment within minutes. He opened the front door, and that's as far as they got. Patrick pressed her up against the wall and lowered his head to capture her lips. She tilted to meet him and growled in appreciation when they connected. His lips were soft, but the kiss was hard with urgency. She parted her mouth and welcomed his tongue while burying her hands in his thick hair and tugging on it, encouraging him to deepen the kiss. Reeve moved her hips forward, and as if in sync, Patrick did too. His arousal pressed against her belly, and she broke off the kiss.

"I can't believe this is really happening," she panted.

"Me either," Patrick said between kisses that he traced from the corner of her mouth and along her neck. She tilted her head back, giving him more access. He brushed her long auburn hair behind her shoulder and gently bit down on at the juncture of her neck and shoulder. His canines just barely broke the skin. The act of dominance triggered waves of lust.

"Wait, I don't even know you, and what about Aster?" she asked, trying to retain a grip on reality and not be consumed by her emotions. Reeve's voice shook as she struggled to form the words.

Patrick groaned, but raised his head to meet her gaze with glowing eyes, his irises darker slits, echoing her struggle for control as his cat called to hers. "Trust me, Aster needs her space, and honestly, I don't think I can stop. We will get to know each other—we have our entire lives to learn everything there is to know and so much more."

He kissed her again, and Reeve allowed her cat closer to the surface. She shifted enough to allow her hands to transform into paws tipped with sharp claws, and she shredded Patrick's shirt. He growled with approval, his eyes flashing golden again right before he sliced her shirt open with an equally sharp set of claws. Soon their shredded clothes lay in a pile on the floor, and they stood naked before each other without any shyness.

Reeve admired her mate, running a hand down his muscular chest and stomach. He had a few scars on his side—faint claw marks that had faded to white—which she guessed were from an old injury. Leaning forward, she gently licked the scars, then placed a soft kiss on his skin. His scent filled her nose, and her whole body pulsed with a powerful wave of arousal. She gasped and stood up straight, almost dizzy with need. Patrick looked her over appreciatively, and her skin flushed under his gaze. His nostrils flared, and his eyes glowed amber right before he spun Reeve around so she faced the wall.

"I don't have the patience to be gentle or slow, but I promise the next time . . ." He ran his nose along her neck and cupped her breasts from behind. She arched her back and pressed into his hands. With every touch, she felt her hold on reality slipping, her conscience suppressed by the call to mate. Every nerve in her body hummed with promise and came alive with each caress.

She whimpered as she stopped resisting. "Take me. I'm yours."

The moment he entered her, Reeve knew there would never be another man for her. Their souls merged, and she felt his need as acutely as her own. His hard, muscular body pressed her against the wall, and she pushed back against him, causing him to drive deeper.

"Oh my God," Reeve cried out, and her knees threatened to go soft.

Patrick brushed her hair aside and bit down on her neck. This time his teeth pierced her skin, completing his claim on her. An overwhelming sense of peace and pleasure consumed her as she felt her blood surging into his mouth. With a final thrust and grunt, Patrick stilled and rode out her orgasm while licking the bite mark clean. They stayed pressed against each other, their pulses pounding, for a few moments, catching their breaths. Reeve slowly turned around to face her mate. His hair stuck out in all directions, and his cheeks were flushed from exertion. Reeve wrapped her arms around his neck and stood on her tiptoes, pulling him to her for a kiss. Now that the initial itch had been scratched, the urgency had waned, but after a few strokes of her tongue, Patrick was ready again.

This time they faced each other. She raised a leg and hooked it over his hip, and he slid inside. They moved in sync, creating a rhythm that quickly rose to a crescendo. Patrick lifted her up, so she wrapped her legs around him. From this angle, she was at the right height to stake her claim. She licked the spot on his neck first, and the vein pulsed underneath her tongue. Her canines dropped, and she struck, drawing his blood into her mouth. The iron-rich warmth bubbled up, and she drank deeply until Patrick released with a muffled groan. Then she retracted her teeth and licked the wound. She was his, and he was hers. The mating bond was officially complete, and there was no going back.

After they collapsed in Patrick's bed, sated and drowsy, the guilt set in.

"I don't regret finding you, my mate," Patrick said as they lay in his dark bedroom. "But I just hate that Aster is hurt. I do care for her, but now, you're all I can see."

"I know. I tried to resist, but the mating call . . . I've never experienced anything so powerful before. Poor Aster." Reeve sighed and rolled over onto her side to face Patrick. He moved so she could settle against him with his arm tucked in behind her, holding her close. "It's not like I planned this. Trust me, I have enough complications in my life, and I just added another reason for my sister to hate me forever."

PURCHASE *FATE, Love & Loyalty* at your favorite book retailer.

www.ingramcontent.com/pod-product-compliance
Lightning Source LLC
Chambersburg PA
CBHW051958170626
46808CB00007B/2678